HOW DESPICABLE
JOE SMITH
MET
HIS MAKER

PALMETTO

P U B L I S H I N G

Charleston, SC

www.PalmettoPublishing.com

"Lattie" the Loggerhead sea turtle statue belongs to the Latitude 32 shop, on Tybee, and was painted by the Artist, Kelley Quigley Friedland, and installed in August 2008.

Hardcover ISBN: 979-8-8229-3261-6

Paperback ISBN: 979-8-8229-3262-3

eBook ISBN: 979-8-8229-3263-0

HOW DESPICABLE JOE SMITH MET HIS MAKER

AMY S. JOHNSTON

Do or do not.
There is no try

~ Yoda

A huge thank you to Marc for his encouragement,
creating an environment where it was possible
for me to concentrate and create and write
and for all his knowledge of planes and guns and stuff.

PRELUDE

Rick's arm is tightening around my neck. I'm seeing stars as I gasp for air. The glaring overhead light in the boat house glints off the knife he's holding to my throat. I can hear his heavy, rasping breath as he strains against my struggles, whispering in my ear:

You should've left it alone, you stupid BITCH!

The intimacy of his whispered words in my ear shatters with the boom of his voice.

She deserved to DIE and I deserved to be the one to take her life. You know I did. She owed me at least that much after what she did to my child. That stupid, fucking BITCH!

He's pleading now: Why couldn't you have just left things alone and let me have that one, sweet moment of justice.

He's starting to cry. His voice is shaking and I feel the wet of his tears on my face. I can smell the desperation on his stale breath as his soft lips move against my cheek; the knife's edge stinging my skin as he presses the point into my neck. A warm trickle snakes down my throat, pooling at my collar bone. If I wasn't about to pass out, I might've tried to offer him some words of comfort for the deep and desperate pain I knew he must be suffering. His wife, Lisa, had once been my friend but she had done some things neither Rick nor I could ever forgive. The thought of what Rick imagined his child had suffered at her hands was too much for this otherwise kind and gentle soul to bear.

What Lisa had done was truly horrifying. The stuff of nightmares that not even a Hollywood movie producer could envision. In all honesty, I couldn't even bring myself to really blame Rick for what he'd done to Lisa, slicing her throat and stabbing her in the heart, twisting the knife deep inside her.

But at this moment, all I'm feeling is an all-consuming sadness for myself.

Rick had murdered his wife for the things she'd done. I had quite literally stumbled over her and been a curious participant in the investigation into her death, discovering the one piece of information that ultimately led Sheriff Bentley and me back to Rick. Now Rick was cornered for his own horrifying deed. And, however, justified it might've been, he had to know in this moment of truth, his own life was now forfeit.

I felt his hot, wet breath in my ear, his spit on my face as he whispered so intimately what he felt he now must do to me for thwarting his revenge.

I also began to cry. For the first time in my 55 years, I was finally living the life I'd always imagined with Marc, the man of my dreams. And because I just couldn't quench my insatiable curiosity and let go of the nagging mystery of Lisa's murder, I was now about to lose it all.

Like a boa constrictor, his arm twisted ever tighter as I clawed my fingers into the muscles of his forearm, trying to loosen his grip. I was desperate for one small breath. I felt something soft snap in my neck, a sharp stab of searing hot pain flared in my shoulder and shot down my right arm. Stars flashed in front of my eyes as I desperately tried to suck in air. I was just about to lose consciousness when I thought I heard one distinctive elongated click.

Just. The. One. Metallic. Click. And oh my god! It was the most beautiful sound in all the whole world. I froze as my heart leapt out of my stomach and into my throat as Rick pivoted to turn and face the source of the sound. He slung me around like a limp rag doll, my feet flying off the floor. The weight of my body threw him off balance for a split second and the only thing I can remember is the feel of his body suddenly going rigid, his legs behind me beginning to shake and to buckle and all of a sudden I could gulp in lungs full of sweet fresh air as his left arm went limp. As Rick began to fall backwards, my legs gave way underneath me and I fell to the deck on both knees, catching myself with my hands as I suddenly fell freely forward. I was gasping for air and sobbing as I craned my head over my left shoulder to look behind me at Rick. His dead eyes looked right at me as the blood from the single gunshot in the middle of his forehead pulsed blood.

I started shaking uncontrollably as a pair of strong hands gripped my shoulders and lifted me up and set me on my feet. I collapsed into the strong steady arms of Marc as Sheriff Bentley brushed past us to Rick's body. I didn't need to see the Sheriff check his pulse. I knew Rick was dead. I buried my face in Marc's chest and started sobbing hysterically to which my knight very gently and lovingly said:

Buck up soldier. It's over and you're OK.

To which I offered him my middle finger.

But that's a story for another time.

CHAPTER 1

The story I think you're here to interview me about is how Marc and I came to be involved in yet another murder investigation. This time Marc would wind up in the hospital, we'd both be held in jail, questioned as suspects and Marc would finally discover our Gidgie Girl can talk. But that all happens later. Let me back up and start at the beginning.

CHAPTER 2

Truth be told, if it weren't for the random administration of God's laws governing the weather patterns of our beautiful, little blue marble which caused hurricane Michael to change its course last minute, despicable Joe Smith might still be alive.

But, God in his infinite wisdom, long ago set into motion the rules that govern our world. And He knew even back then that this late October hurricane would make landfall from the Gulf of Mexico, push northward up into Mississippi and Alabama and suddenly change course and head across the whole width of Georgia, barreling straight for the little sliver of our coast with its fragile tiny group of barrier islands. Caught in the cross hairs of nature's fury, Michael would dump its waning strength on Tybee Island and give cover to the nefarious deed of someone who decided it was high time Joe Smith met his Maker.

So, in a way, it could be said that Joe's death was not only predestined but even God's will. Well, maybe God's will is a bit of a stretch.

Certainly, man's will had a little something to do with it. God's opportunity, man's motive and means and Joe's own culpability led to what happened in that late October and forever changed the lives of so many in our little corner of paradise.

If Belinda Carlisle is right and heaven is a place on earth, then it exists at 32.015° N, -80.884° E and is known as Tybee Island. snuggled cheek by jowl with its barrier island siblings just off the Georgia coast, toes barely dipping in the water of the Atlantic,

Tybee is both a city and an island, part of our nation's national seashore, protected by the Georgia Department of Natural Resources. The north side of the island is a natural wonder with Feral horses free ranging pristine beaches, chasing each other along lazy sandy paths lined with ancient cypress trees, branches heavy under the weight of Spanish moss and late summer southern humidity so thick its enough to make you sweat like a prostitute in church. Rolling dunes of sea oats frame the loggerhead sea turtles' ancient nesting grounds.

The south side of the island is dominated by Tybee Island Village, where most of us year rounders live on shady live oak lined lanes in pastel colored, clapboard cottages, a sleepy little southern town of entrepreneurs and eccentrics, trying to all live peaceably together. US highway 80 (also known as Butler Street) is the main two-lane road through town on which most of the village's businesses reside along with the Sherriff's office and jail, a courthouse, town hall and the village library where all our community meetings are held. Right off the town square in a little, gravel covered alcove is Hucapoos diner and dive bar, community central owned and run by the Hucapoo sisters, Louise and Mikki. It share's the alcove space with the Inferno Hot Sauce shop, the post office, a bohemian pottery studio (that also sells hand tie-died souvenir t-shirts) and a single screen movie theater where the most current showing is always 3 months old.

Tybee is the place where dreams are lived out as dolphins harass the migrating herons and gators lay in wait in the marshlands of the back bay. Marc calls it paradise. I call it home, which is my word for paradise.

Marc and I are not married but we've been together a long time, having found each other late in our lives. Marc long freed from an unhappy first marriage that miraculously produced two of the most amazing human beings I've ever known, his son, Tyler, and his daughter, Anne. I credit Marc with their amazingness. He's calm and brilliant and funny and charming. The thought would never occur to him that there is anything he can't do and I love how he lives his life by the seat of his pants, thriving on adventure, calculated risks and controlled danger. His nickname around the island is Indiana Johnson and I can't imagine two kids growing up with a better father.

My marriage wasn't exactly a disaster but we produced no legacies. My husband was both brilliant and incredibly stupid. Refusing to acknowledge any human frailty or to take proper care of himself and his congenital heart condition, he died suddenly – but not unexpectedly – of a blood clot that went to his brain. So, widowed I was for many years until Marc found me and lured me back to the world of the living.

Marc and I, now in our mid-fifties and at a certain place in our lives, free to make some different choices for no one but ourselves, decided what we both really wanted was to pursue our dreams of living on Tybee Island, me writing my mystery novels and Marc flying his motor glider, teaching young daredevils to fly and letting thrill seeking tourists hurl themselves out of his Cessna Caravan at 10,000 feet. We never asked ourselves: Why. Only why not and picked up and immigrated to Paradise.

So, last Thursday and all through Friday, Hurricane Michael blew across Georgia and barreled right toward Tybee Island and resolved a lot of problems for more than a few of the locals. One such resolution was to the problem of my married stalker, Morgan Stephenson, when the idiot decided to ride out the storm on his charter fishing boat and was unceremoniously washed out to sea within the first hour after Michael roared across the Old Romery Marshland, crossed Wassaw Sound and skidded to a shuddering stop right on top of Tybee. Problem solved!

The other resolution came in the form of the death of Joe Smith, a wholly despicable human being who Marc frequently said needed killing. And God said, vengeance is mine. Vengeance coming in the form of a fortuitous four by four cedar fence plank hurled like a spear into Joe's noggin at 50 plus miles an hour. Again, problem solved!

Well, one problem solved. Another created when Dirk Bentley – Chatham County sheriff - decided Joe's death needed a little more investigating. Dirk used to run a holistic detective agency over in Savannah but went out of business two years ago when he focused a little too much on ghost, horror, time travel cases. After a long dark tea time in bankruptcy, he too decided Tybee Island held the key to his future and sure enough the locals saw it too and elected him sheriff of Chatham County. All in, he's a good-natured man of integrity, a barrel chested, 6'4", gun toting, second amendment, older gentleman with a quirky sense of humor and a head full of thick snow white hair and a bristly bottle brush mustache to match. A man who Marc and I both respect immensely and trust implicitly.

Listen Dirk...sorry...um I mean Sherriff...the proximate cause of death was the four by four, case closed. Problem solved.

Well now I ain't so sure about that, Miss Amy. Last night I had this vision, see..

I'm standing on the beach, ankle deep in sand, my arms wrapped around my shivering body, trying to shout to be heard above the whipping wind that is the dying gasp of Michael on Tybee. The Sheriff is also shouting a little too close to my ear but I think I just heard him say he'd had a vision.

Oh god!

Yes, exactly. See, Joe was a wholly despicable human being.

Yes, Yes he was.

And you and Marc know that just about better than anyone. What with Rodney being ya'lls close friend and all.

Uh huh…

And I believe it's fair to say there are more than a few folks around here who would've liked to see ole Joe get what he so might've richly deserved, see…

Uh huh…

And this here storm that just blew through, well maybe that's just a bit of fortuitous cover, if you see what I mean.

mmmhmmm…

See what I mean?

No…. Dirk. Listen. Four by Four to the head….

About that… kinda' strange don't you think?

Sheriff, let me ask you something.

Shoot.

No, I don't want to shoot you just yet. I just want to know why you are looking at this as anything other than a storm related death?

Well, it's that vision you see. Joe, well he himself came to me last night and told me I oughta be lookin' pretty close at anything strange I might come across. Then he turns up dead. Counts as strange in my book. And that four by four lodged straight up in his melon like that,

45 degree angle, not exactly natural. Maybe he was hit with it first, knocked down or unconscious, and then the pointy end of that there board rammed in his scull. The death blow as it were.

And you're sure it wasn't all those extra-large, double strong cherry bombs you and Marc had at Hucapoo's last night that maybe gave you your nocturnal vision? Marc wandered home pretty lit…assuming you probably did too.

I only had me just the two bombs and my visions only come to me when someone needs me to investigate somethin', as you well know. Now, Miss Amy, tell me again how you came to find Joe.

Um, well, earlier tonight shortly after midnight, Marc's phone rang. It was Rodney.

And is Rodney in the habit of calling' ya'll in the middle of the night?

I wouldn't say habit exactly. But, sometimes he needs something or other and Joe was never very good to Rodney, as you know. Marc has always been more like a brother to Rodney and so Rodney calls Marc.

Uh huh, go on.

Anyway, Marc said Rodney was upset because it was so late and Joe wasn't home and Rodney had been having seizures and needed his medicine and couldn't find it. Rodney takes some pretty frequent doses of Phenobarbital and other drugs and God only knows if there was even any of it in the house. Joe's been known to sell Rodney's pills for cash.

mmmhmm.

So, Marc decided to go over and check on Rodney.

But how did you come to be walking the north beach in the middle of the night to even find Joe?

Well, I'm pretty restless at night and Marc was going over to Rodney's and I just decided to get up too. A little later, Marc called me to say Joe and the meds were MIA. Marc was calling one of his old air force buddies who works over at the Tuxedo Pharmacy and see if he could get his hands on a few pills to get Rodney through the night. I didn't expect Marc to be home anytime soon and I can never sleep without him in the bed anyway. So, I just decided I'd take a long walk on the beach and see if I could make myself tired enough to get sleepy. I was just walking along. I always have my flashlight with me at night so I can try and watch out for the turtles and not disturb their nests. And I almost stumbled over Joe's feet sticking out of the sea oats over there.

I pointed in the direction of Joe's Size 11 sneakers.

Flashlight huh?

Well, yeah. I know we're not supposed to use flashlights on the beach at night during loggerhead nesting season, but I didn't want to risk stumbling into a nest or stepping on and crushing a baby turtle.

Fair enough. Did you go into the dunes or go anywhere near the body or touch it or anything?

No, Those Zazzle size 11 red swirl high tops are pretty distinctive, so I knew without having to look to close who it was. I always have my cell with me and I called 911 and – abracadabra – here you are.

OK. Well, listen, I'm gonna want you to come down to the station later today and let Lucy take down your statement and I'm sure the county prosecutor will want to talk to you. So, just make sure you don't go off the island, OK?

Wait! What? Why? Til when? I've got a meeting with my publisher in New York in a few days.

Um, no ma'am. Not now you don't. You need to stay on island until further notice.

Dirk, please come on. You know I can't miss this meeting. You and everyone else on this island knows my last book was a flop and I need to bend over backwards to keep my publisher happy. I can't miss this meeting, Dirk.

Panic is rising rapidly in me. Writing is how I make my living and for me (financially) it's literally publish or perish. Stephen King I'm not so I am dependent many times on the good graces of my publisher to keep me going.

Miss Amy, please try to understand. You know that you and Marc are usually up to your necks in most things that go on on Tybee. Your story…

My story? …

Your account of the events leading to your discovery of the deceased seems straight up and you've always been a pretty straight forward kinda lady. But, you can see how it looks when the last two - that's right, I said it – twwooo (Sheriff Bentley holds up and waggles the first two fingers of his right hand in my face for emphasis) dead bodies on this island were both just happened upon by you. Now don't go rollin' your eyes at me, missy. As the Chatham County sheriff, I'm asking you real polite like to stay on island until me and the county prosecutor can figure this thing out. Please don't make me have to place you in custody just to get you to cooperate.

I'm flabbergasted. I'm speechless. I'm highly annoyed. I'm chilled in the night ocean winds, stomach growling. It's never really cold on Tybee, but the night winds off the Atlantic at this time of year can chill you enough to justify a jacket, which I'm not wearing over my usual thin plain white t-shirt. I need food and I want coffee and to talk to Marc. What Dirk was saying made perfect sense. He was doing his duty and he was right that I had been the one to discover the last two bodies found dead on Tybee.

I don't know why, but I tend to find myself in some - shall we say – unusual situations from time to time and Marc is forever having to help me out of them. Let's just say his military training and fearlessness has come in handy a time or two. And because he loves me, he sticks around and tries to keep me (and Rodney) out of trouble. We're his penance for some undisclosed past life deeds, covered by our relationship's statute of limitations.

OK. FINE! But when my publisher screams a blue streak about missing my meeting, I'm giving him your phone number. And my agent isn't going to be too happy either.

I'm telling you to stay on the island, period. Just remember, I've got a nice comfy cell waiting for an occupant if you try to bounce and leave Tybee. I mean it Amy, no disappearing act like the last time. Understood?

Understood.

Do I have your word?

Yeeees.

Do I need to tell Marc?

Noooo.

OK. Now why don't you head on back home and try to get some rest. Better still, be thinking of how you're gonna tell Marc you found yet another body. Do you want me to get my deputy to escort you or can you get home on your own?

I'm not a child, Dirk.

Yes, ma'am, but you are a lady out alone and it's still the middle of the night and pitch dark out. Marc would have my plumbs in a basket if I let anything happen to you.

I'll be fine. I'll just go back the way I came.

OK. Now you be sure and call me if you stumble over any more bodies along the way, ya hear?

Ha Ha very funny. You're an idiot, you know that?

Yes ma'am, I surely do. Wife reminds me every day.

CHAPTER 3

By the time I make my way back to our home, I'm feeling a little tired and my leg muscles are hurting from trying to walk upright in the sugar soft sand. I let myself in without a key. You don't need keys on Tybee. In fact, you can always tell tourists from the locals by the way they always lock up everything. We natives don't lock things, there's no need. It's an island!

So, I let myself in and Gidget is sitting right at the front door where I left her, waiting for me to return. She'd never leave her post until both Marc and I are safely home and under her watchful protection.

Hey Gidgie girl. I'm back. I'm sorry I'm keeping you up all night.

I pat her on the head and she gives me a soulful look of complete annoyance. She does not like to be kept up at night and she's a little out of sorts with our nocturnal activity.

Did I mention Gidget is a very unusual dog. She's a beautiful, snow white, 3 year old Great Pyrenees with big soulful brown eyes trimmed with long white fairy eyelashes. She was once used as a bate dog in a dog fighting ring. Rescued by the Chatham County Sherriff's department and the local ASPCA a year ago when the ring was busted, the shelter gave her to Marc and me to foster. She was in tough shape and practically torn to pieces, sick with every disease a dog can get. The county shelter vet thought the merciful thing to do was to put her down. But, Marc and I begged the leader of the rescue group to let us give her a chance to live.

About a week after she came to us, I was sitting at the kitchen table working on my most recent flop, Gidget laying a few feet away, when she suddenly got up, came to my side, put her paw on my knee and looked me right in my eyes and said:

"I've decided I can live here".

It's funny thinking back on that now. It didn't even really phase me that she'd spoken actual words. I didn't dare tell anyone about it, given my history. But, it didn't matter, Gidget told me she's just as happy to keep it our little secret and let the universe sort it all out in due course.

Not only did she live, she thrived. When I took her back to the shelter a month later for a checkup, the vet thought she was the wrong dog. All the shelter staff came into the exam room to see the "new" Gidget, oohs and aahs all around, hugs and kisses abounding, pictures taken for the shelter's website to show what miracles could be wrought with donations for rescue and rehabilitation. Gidget absolutely absorbed every last ounce of affection proffered.

Since then, she's become quite a little celebrity in her own right, famous in our little corner of paradise for her rapid and stunning recovery. She has transformed herself into a gorgeous specimen and is more like all of Tybee's dog, our symbol of beauty and resilience.

Often she reminds me she's really meant to be a show dog, and so I take her for rides in my jeep or for walks around the island, no leash needed. She belongs to the spirit of the island and it belongs to her.

People may not know my name but they surely know Gidget on sight and will stop us on the street to greet her. More than once I've reintroduced myself to someone as Gidget's "mommy" only then to be remembered. Usually, when we're well out of ear shot she'll tell me what each one smelled like, where they'd been and what they'd been up to. Let's just say there are some things better left unknown about some folks.

I take her everywhere I go. She rides in my yellow Jeep Wrangler like a person buckled in the front seat. She's calm and well behaved and welcome in every island establishment, especially Huca poo's diner, where I have to insist that The Sisters (Micki and Louise Huca poo) who own the joint not sneak her pizza bites on the sly. By the way, The Sisters make the best griddle breakfast on island and if ever I wake up in the morning and find Marc is already up and gone, I know where to find him.

But, Gidget knows how to fight to survive from her days in the dog fighting pit. And while she's normally very calm and sweet and gentle, she is also highly protective of us and she and Marc have formed a mutually beneficial alliance designed to try and keep me out of trouble. Marc once told Gidget she was in charge of me whenever he was not around and then he looked at me, laughed a little and winked, saying:

"she's just a doggie, she understands exactly nothing I am saying".

…to which Gidget responded with her own little wink because, of course, she understood exactly everything he said. If only Marc knew the joke was really on him.

In the same way I don't like to be too far away from Marc, Gidget won't leave my side and will not let me out of her sight unless she has no choice. Like tonight when I went for my walk about.

It's still loggerhead nesting season on Tybee Island, until about the end of October. While the momma turtles dug their last nests and laid their last clutch of eggs sixty days or so ago, in late October, the babies are still hatching, digging their way to the surface and struggling to the sea. The last thing they need is a 100 pound hair ball standing between them and survival. So, Gidget very reluctantly agreed to stay behind and warm a spot in the front hall, warning me if I was gone too long, I'd better watch where I stepped when I came home.

I'd grabbed my flashlight and left her by the front door and walked out into the night wind, discovering Joe.

But I'm back now and as I dust the sand off my feet in the little half bathroom by the front door and grab my shawl hanging on the hook. Gidget informs me she thought she heard a hoard of zombies in the back garden earlier. Now she didn't see 'em, but she knows they were there and, deeming it bark worthy, proceeded to scare them off by barking her head off for about fifteen minutes. And, oh yeah, the neighbors came out and yelled too, so that helped. I sigh and wrap myself tightly against the chill I'm feeling and decide I'm actually too tired now to think about how annoyed Tim and Cheryl might be from all the barking and I'll go apologize to them tomorrow.

Marc isn't home yet and I'd only left on one light in the front hall when I lit out for my impromptu walk. I'm very bonded with Marc and I feel so much happier when I'm with him. I know he's just down the beach a way, seeing about Rodney, but it's now after two am and the house feels dark and empty. And I feel more than a little apprehensive about telling him about Joe, especially the part about how I was the one who found him. There was that other time I was involved in a murder investigation, having quite literally stumbled over the body of my friend, Lisa. As then, Marc is not going to be happy to find I was the one who discovered yet another lifeless body.

And, too, I feel more than a little sad, thinking about telling Marc about it being Joe I found because Marc will most likely be the one to tell Rodney that his only living family and caretaker, his uncle, is gone, knowing Rodney's future on Tybee is now very, very uncertain.

At seventy years old, I'm sure Joe never expected to have to be the primary care giver for his disabled, epileptic nephew. And, in all fairness, it's not easy to be responsible for every aspect of another person's life and well-being. Add to that Joe's age and his own failing health and their severe lack of funds for basic needs, making their life together an untenable situation, at best. More than once, Marc has seen a need in their household and stepped in to help bridge the gap a little. I never bothered too much about that, my problem with Joe stemmed from the seeming indifference Joe had to Rodney's basic physical needs and care.

And, I disliked him intensely for my own personal reasons, too. Early last summer Joe had come to our home uninvited and unexpected and tried to kiss me and force himself on me. Joe being the reprobate he was, tried this in Marc's home when he thought Marc was out flying. The weather that day had not been great and Marc had come home early and found Joe pinning me to the kitchen floor. Marc is 5'7", wirey, very strong and all muscle. Plus his military training makes him lethal, especially when he's mad and protecting what belongs to him. To this day, I don't like to think what might've happened if – once again – the weather hadn't played a role in the outcome. Well, the weather and my cast iron frying skillet, which sent Joe to the hospital with a well-deserved concussion.

Over the years, there have been many times when Marc and I would take our evening walk along the beach and wind up at their rusty little trailer that sits right on the edge of Tybee's most valuable piece of undeveloped beach real estate only to find Rodney alone and several days removed from his last bath. With clothes so ripe you could smell them from the front door, Marc would make me wait outside on the front stoop while he got Rodney into the shower, scrubbed then dressed him in his own shirt and pants, walking home in nothing but his Mac Weldon's. This became such a frequent occurrence that I started carrying a t-shirt and shorts in my straw bag so Marc would have something to wear home.

That rusty little trailer is quite possibly the most valuable home on the island given that it resides on Tybee's most desirable piece of undeveloped real estate. But for the fact that it sits at the top of a hill on the north side of the island, overlooking a sloping dune of sea oats rolling down to a beach used for eons as primary nesting grounds by the protected loggerhead sea turtles. I think I mentioned that Tybee is actually an island, part of our nation's national seashore and is a protected area managed by the Georgia Department of Natural Resources. So, even though Joe and Rodney own the little acre of land the trailer sits on, they can never sell it or engage with any Trumpster's to develop it in any way shape or form. In fact, it's illegal under the Georgia Shore Protection Act to even walk on the dunes where the sea oats are growing. So, the richest men on island are actually dirt poor, living off of Rodney's social security disability income and what little retirement Joe has from his former deep sea fishing days.

But now, I'm safely back in our cozy cottage and I've decided to go upstairs and get in bed. Gidget wants to know where I've been and what I've seen. She says I smell faintly of salty sea air and dead body.

What the hell, momma?

Yeah, long story, Gidgie girl. I'll tell you tomorrow. Let's go to bed.

She needs no real prompting to lead the way up the darkened stairs. I've left the light on in the front hall for Marc and follow Gidget. By the time I drag myself up the stairs, she's already entered our bedroom and plopped down loudly onto the floor in the far corner of the bedroom.

After I've changed my clothes and brushed my teeth, I climb stiffly into bed, curl myself around Marc's pillow which has his deeply comforting smell all over it and wrap myself in the cottony down of the duvet. I immediately drift into a deep, relaxing sleep. The only thing I remember hearing was the contented sigh of Gidget finally being able to settle down for the night.

CHAPTER 4

I'm floating in the ocean, rocking back and forth, up and down on a gentle wave, and in this lovely dream, I open my eyes and see a clear blue sky above and the bright sun hurts my eyes. I look around me at the foamy sea, pink and silky soft and I'm thinking, wait, that's not right. The ocean isn't pink. Why is the ocean pink? And it slowly dawns on me that not only is the ocean not pink, I'm not floating in the ocean, I'm lying on my back in our bed and the gentle rocking motion is caused by Marc lying between my legs, penetrating me. I love morning sex and so does Marc and it's not that unusual for me to wake up with him laying on top of me, kissing me and pushing into me. It's my favorite way to start my day. But, its also a little disorienting since I don't remember Marc coming home from seeing about Rodney. Normally, he'd at least come into our bedroom, wake me with a kiss and say he's home.

But it doesn't matter and as we move into our long ago found rhythm, the train of my thoughts jumps the tracks. It's another glorious morning in paradise and I'm with the man of my dreams and I have some writing to do after breakfast. It dawns on me for the millionth time how - for the first time in my life – I feel truly content. Marc finishes with me and kisses me on my neck and rolls off of me and we lay in bed next to each other, breathing heavily. After a few minutes, Gidget stirs from a spot at the opposite end of the room and I listen to her nails click across the hardwood floor to Marc's side of the bed. She wants him to get up and let her out, which he does dutifully without complaint, and that's my que to get up and go downstairs, feed her and see about our breakfast.

When I'm showered and dressed, teeth brushed and shoes on, I come downstairs and suggest to Marc we go down to "The Sisters" for our Saturday morning breakfast. Again, The Sisters own a diner known as Huca poo's and their forte is bites and booze, the best thin crust cheese pizza ever baked by mankind and double strong cherry bombs. They also open early six days a week (not Sunday because the Sisters are very faithful) and they make the best gridle breakfast east of Eden.

Huca poo's is community central and is the one place on Tybee where everyone goes to know everyone else's business. It's almost always packed with Chatham County's sheriff's deputies, signifying it is the single finest eating establishment in all the County. It's a beloved island institution that everyone frequents almost every day, partly because of the tremendous food and atmosphere but also to support The Sisters. The two are deeply loved by the island, two older ladies who long ago sunk their life savings and more into a failing business, transforming it into something that defines Tybee and holds us all together. Louise is the older sister and chief cook and bottle washer. Micki is the younger sister who raised her only daughter all by herself, the father long ago having abandoned them both to the vagaries of life alone in this world.

The Sisters work hard, support themselves, take no guff and employ every wayward soul subsisting on the island that they can afford.

The Sisters have always focused their talents on cooking and taking care of their customers. So, it's been the locals who have decorated the place. It's covered in posters spouting the wisdom of beer. Like: "Beer – turning bow into wow" and "Beer – helping white guys dance since 1842". Old, faded photos and concert posters of Janice Joplin and Jimmy Hendricks hang crookedly under a sunglass-wearing steer skull mounted inside over the front door.

There's always music playing from somewhere and fall is a time for nonstop rowdy Georgia Tech football gatherings. Every time Marc and I go in there, he tees up Southern Culture On The Skids on the sound system and that damn Camel Walk song he's so enamored of. Oh my god! I can never get those damn lyrics out of my head:

"Baby, would you eat that there snack cracker in
your special outfit for me please?"
Or this one:
"Say, you don't think there's any way I can get that
quarter from underneath your pointy boot, do ya?

Marc loves this band and when he hears <u>Camel Walk</u>, I can depend on him repeating these lyrics to me at least a thousand times. He'll work them into every conversation we have until I threaten to start calling his motor glider, Fraulein princess...which bugs the shit out of him for some unknown reason. It was engineered and born in Germany nearly 40 years ago and I believe it is the true love of his life.

Huca poo's is actually quite large with a big outdoor beer deck, seating areas with overstuffed couches and chairs patrons are careful not to ruin with spilled beer or food out of respect for The Sisters. And over large blue leather corner booths. It has a cozy, claustrophobic feel from all the concert posters and memorabilia plastering the walls and ceiling. It's the heart of the island and Marc and I love it and the Sisters.

My ulterior motive for suggesting Huca poos to Marc for our breakfast this morning is to find out the latest scuttle butt on Joe's death. I haven't yet told Marc about Joe or that I'm the one who found his body. I figured I'd let Marc find out like everyone else on Tybee… by word of mouth. Why ruin a perfectly good Saturday morning with the unpleasantness of last night?

When I suggested breakfast with The Sisters, Marc almost couldn't contain his unadulterated joy, the relief in his eyes almost made me laugh out loud. I readily admit I'm not a good cook (or really any kind of cook) and to say Marc likes the Sisters' cooking is an understatement. He's almost salivating with the anticipation of the taste of their maple sugar cured, thick cut, extra crispy bacon. When he sees the look on my face, he mistakes my suppressed laughter for upset and pats me on the shoulder consolingly and tells me not to worry about my lack of kitchen skills because apparently only The Sisters truly know how to scramble an egg. And anyway I'm skilled in other rooms where it equally counts. And you know what, I'm actually fine with this assessment and I grab my straw bag and my sun hat and off we go. We leave Gidget snoring quietly in her daytime bed in the family room, her tummy full of kibble and dreaming of chasing hummngbirds and dragonflies.

CHAPTER 5

Huca poo's is buzzing this morning. Every deputy on Tybee is having breakfast all at once, in addition to some locals, a few tourists still hanging around after the end of the summer season and I see a couple of Department of Natural Resources employees sitting at the counter. The sign at the door says: Wait To Be Seated, but the Sisters are way too busy this morning to be meeting, greeting and seating. So, as all of us islanders know when it's uber busy like this, it's grab the first free seat and wait to catch one of the waitresses in passing. Marc and I grab the only two empty stools at the counter, one on either side of the DNR dudes. Micki comes rushing out with a tray full of heaping plates of steamy hot bacon and eggs and a basket of homemade honey biscuits, delivering them to a nearby table of four deputies. She returns behind the ancient red formica counter and seeing me, turns my coffee mug right side up (she knows I need my coffee fix first thing), takes a napkin roll of silverware from the front pocket of her apron and drops it in front of me and says:

Hey darlin'? Had kind of a late night last night I hear.

I look up into her azure blue eyes and shake my head ever so slightly by way of begging her not to say any more. She nods imperceptibly, winks at me and knows exactly what I mean. Because, truth be told, Micki and Louise Huca poo have "the gift" and in that one second of my strong emotional panic, she caught my signal and understood I hadn't yet told Marc what must've already been disclosed to her by at least one of Sherriff Bentley's deputies.

Marc is sitting two seats away on the other side of the DNR dudes so I don't think he heard Micki ask me about last night.

OK sweetie. Whatcha' havin'?

We'll have Marc's usual.

That's all I need to say for Micki to know what I'm ordering. Small breakfast off the kids' menu: One fried egg over medium, one piece of bacon extra crispy, one biscuit - hold the butter and jam – and a small OJ… We eat it every single time we come into Huca poo's for breakfast, without exception.

Honestly, angel, I ain't never seen such a skinny, muscular man eat so little and be so hyper. But, whatever. Comin up.

Well, maybe better ask him first, just on the off chance he wants something different this morning. I think he likes to be asked, at least.

Micki laughs and bustles back into the kitchen, yelling for Louise to hear: two Indiana Johnson's, medium.

The DNR guys finish their last mouthfuls, drop a ten spot on the counter – cost of breakfast for two plus a tip, no bill required – and get up and leave. The burly officer next to me, nods toward me and says:

Ma'am.

I nod my head and say, "Mornin."

He picks up his hat and leaves, his, comrade following close behind. Most of the other patrons have either finished their breakfast and left or are making to leave. You can tell when it's a local who is getting ready to leave because we all stack our dishes in a neat pile on the edge of our tables. And we all always put our condiments and salt and pepper shakers back neatly arranged in the middle of the table with the napkin dispenser. It's our way of sort of busing our own tables and making it easier for the Sisters to clean up after us. Only off-islanders leave their tables a mess.

As soon as the DNR guys are gone, Marc gets up and moves to the stool next to me. The move frees up two side by side stools for an elderly couple who has just come in. They look familiar but I can't recall their names. They are not permanent residents. I think the term for this couple is "snow birds", northerners who migrate south for the winter. Even in mid-October, there are parts of the northeast that are already experiencing nor'easters and blizzard like snow. There'll be many, many more snow birds arriving on Tybee in the next few weeks and they'll crowd the shops and the restaurants during the days between early morning and early afternoon and Marc and I will probably need to adjust our schedules a bit to try and avoid the crowds at certain times of day.

But, I like seeing these older couples. Long married, long comfortable and agreeable, a whole lifetime of shared experiences that have bonded them to each other in a way they can never be bonded with anyone else on this Earth. I sometimes fantasize that Marc and me – that we are they – and that we will one day be cozying up in a Huca poo's booth for dinner at 4 o'clock in the afternoon. We'll see.

Sometimes I think I might like to get married again and I can't imagine anyone I'd rather spend the balance of my days with than

Marc. But he is a free spirit and his deep abiding joy is the freedom of flying things…and jumping out of flying things…and letting others jump out of flying things. Everything about him leaves me unconvinced he'd ever be happy tied down again to one person.

I am Marc's polar opposite, someone who has always had my feet firmly planted on the ground. My super power is my ability to be always reasonable and practical. The thought of Marc making me his wife has probably never even crossed his mind…and probably never will. So, for now, I am content to be content with life as it exists for us.

But one thing Marc will definitely not be happy about is hearing about Joe and that it was I who found his body. With all these Sherriff's deputies in Huca poo's this morning, talking loudly (as men do) about the events of last night, I'm sure he's probably already overheard the only new news on the island this morning. So, I'm just going to sit here, eat the delicious breakfast Micki has just placed in front of me and just wait for the proverbial shit to hit the fan. I take a tentative sip of my steaming hot coffee when Marc turns to me and asks:

So, you didn't actually touch Joe's body last night or anything, right?

Coffee goes down my windpipe and I'm sputtering and coughing when the bell over the restaurant door tinkles and in strides Sherriff Bentley. Suddenly, all the air goes out of the room as every deputy sucks in his gut and quickly woofs down their last morsels of breakfast, pulling a few bills out of their wallets and making like a tree and leaving. Things proceed at a pretty calm, quiet pace here on Tybee, but when Dirk walks into a room, every deputy in uniform is immediately on duty. The place clears out pretty quickly and it winds up being just Marc and me, the older couple on the other side of Marc, the Sherriff and the Sisters.

Dirk strides over to the counter, straddles the stool on the other side of me and now I'm sandwiched between Marc and the giant super cop and I'm thinking the only topic of conversation is about to be my late night meanderings and the discovery of Joe's body. Marc and Dirk begin talking over my head like I'm a child to be ignored.

So, Marc, what time you get home last night?

Mmmm, I think probably between 2:30 and 3am.

Yeah? Any particular reason you out so late?

Yep.

Crickets!

Micki comes back to us with coffee pot in hand. She sees the three of us sitting there, me looking haplessly down at my plate, not eating, her "gift" twitching wildly. She turns on her heal and makes a b-line to fill the cups of the snowbirds without saying a word. She really doesn't need the gift to see two alpha males squaring off.

But Marc is a cool cat. He's not about to make Dirk's job easy for him. He's going to make The Sherriff ask him pointedly where he went, why and can anyone corroborate his whereabouts at roughly midnight to 2 am this morning.

So, where did you go and why and can anyone corroborate your whereabouts at between let's say midnight and 2:00am this morning?

Well, let's see now.

Marc looks at the ceiling, strokes his chin and purses his lips in a comic mimic of someone trying to think real hard.

Now, don't hurt yourself there buddy. Just tell me straight up.

I got a call shortly after midnight from Rodney Smith. Amy can corroborate that. He said Joe hadn't come home and I left shortly after that and went round to see about him. I was in fact on the phone with an old air force buddy of mine who works over at the Tuxedo. That was probably about 1am. Rodney needed a refill of one of his meds pretty desperately. Better to get the meds than wind up in the ER over in Savannah. So, that buddy will verify the time of our call and when he met me at the pharmacy. Rodney will verify when I got back with the meds and when I left to go home. Got home between 2:30 and 3:00 am. Amy was already in bed asleep. She talked to me a bit, but went right back to sleep. OK?

OK.

Of course, Sheriff, you already know Amy's activities and whereabouts last night. Isn't that right, Amy?

Uumm…Uh huh. Gulp!

I'm still looking down at my plate, pretending to discover with my fork what might be hiding under my egg.

So, we can say for sure where you were at the time in question. We know Amy was with you at midnight and shortly after until you left. And, we know what time her call came into 911 – at roughly 1:00 am. What we don't know is Amy's whereabouts and activities from the time you left your home until she called 911.

Wait, What?

Marc is sitting up very straight now and leaning way over in front of me, suddenly aware there's an unspoken threat to what belongs to him.

Well there is close to an hour of her time that is not accounted for.

Now wait just a minute, Dirk.

And, there's the series of unfortunate events that the last two… that's right, I'm going there yet again…twwwooo (first two fingers wagling in my face again) dead bodies on this island were found by you, my dear.

But…

But, nothing

Sheriff, if you're suggesting Amy killed Joe, that's is patently absurd and you are a lunatic. You know she's not physically strong enough to drive a four by four into a man's scull with enough force to lodge it there and kill him. And that's assuming he just stood there and took it…which, Joe – the brawling bully that he was – most certainly would not have done. She'd never do such a thing anyway, even if she could.

Now just hold your horses a minute, Marc. I didn't say I thought she killed him. I'm simply saying there's about an hour of her time un-accounted for. Fortunately, it might not need to be accounted for be-cause the coroner's initial estimated time of death is sometime around midnight, maybe as much as an hour before that. Can't be too much more precise than that right now until the final autopsy results are in because the body was out in the sea oats for some unknown amount of time and that storm did a number on it. But, best as can be determined at this point is, he was dead for some time before Amy found him. And, Amy was with you when that call came in from Rodney shortly after midnight. It would be better if you weren't each other's only alibi, as it were.

Oh, if only Gidget could be our alibi and confirm my whereabouts after Marc left to go see about Rodney. But, a talking dog as my alibi doesn't seem like such a good thing just at the moment.

By the way, can the two of you just stop talking over my head like I'm not sitting right here. And, can you keep your voices down. We're not the only ones in this diner. I roll my eyes and tilt my head toward the snowbirds on the stools next to Marc.

Don't worry about us Miss. We're not listening.

Nice! Comedians.

Ok, well listen. I know the two of you are pretty connected around the island. And, what would be helpful is if you hear anything about this situation, anything at all, even if you don't think it'll be pertinent, you come and tell me. I've talked to Rodney and I know approximately the last time he says he saw Joe at their trailer. So, I've got an estimated window for the time of death. I know the means of death. A four by four jammed in Joe's scull. Given the storm, the location the body was found and the weather, I think it's safe to assume he was killed where he was found. What I don't know is who killed him. I don't need to know the why. That's a worry for the county prosecutor to explain at trial. I just need to find out who and make an arrest.

Gotcha, Dirk. Listen, if we hear anything, we'll let you know. In the meantime, am I still on island arrest or can I reschedule my meeting with my publisher.

No ma'am, you may not. Neither of you may leave this island under ANY circumstances, until we have an arrest and the prosecutor gives you the all clear. And I'm afraid that means you, Marc, are grounded until further notice.

WHAT? Holy hounds of hell, Dirk!

Seriously, Marc, surely even you can see why you're not allowed to just get in a plane and take off? Not to put too fine a point on it, but if you were a suspect, you would be the literal definition of a flight risk. LITERALLY! A FLIGHT RISK! Both of you – on island – until this thing is solved! UNDERSTOOD?

He's on his feet now and almost shouting, one hand resting on the butt of his gun, still holstered, face turning red while he points his giant index finger in my face. I think we understand.

Marc is on his feet now too, about to square off in the escalating alpha dog showdown. I, being the reasonable, practical one put my hands up, one on Marc's chest and one in Dirk's direction and say:

Ok. Alright. We understand. Let's just settle down now boys.

The snowbirds are watching us with amusement. This is probably the most fun they've had in ages.

CHAPTER 6

Look, don't get pissy with me, Marc. It's not my fault you can't fly. I didn't kill Joe. And, I'm missing my meeting with my publisher and that's a problem, too, as you well know.

We are home from Huca poo's and sitting at our kitchen table. I had intended to spend the day on my new manuscript, book four in the Tybee Island mysteries. But Marc wants to talk about last night. Gidget is lying on the floor a few feet away, listening intently, because she also wants to know what I was up to last night. I've just finished outlining the sequence of events that lead me to find Joe's body and to call the Sheriff. Gidget and I can sense Marc's growing agitation and she's becoming very fidgety. Gidget is very attached to Marc – he is her person – and she's very in tune with his moods and tone of voice.

I'm not saying it's your fault, Amy. I'm just annoyed that every time there's a dead body on this island, you're the one who just happens to come across it. And there winds up being all kinds of fallout that gives both of us heartburn. It's downright freaky. It's like you're a magnate for dead bodies. And, now that magnate is costing me flying time and money.

I know. I'm sorry.

Don't say you're sorry for something you're not sorry for!

He's starting to raise his voice - something he rarely ever does – and I hear that tone that means he spent twenty years in the military barking orders to dogface subordinates. Which I – clearly – am not, thank you very much. My practical self is telling my annoyed self to stay reasonable and don't get mad. A solution is what we need, not an argument.

Amy, listen. I have to fly to earn money. Money we use to pay our bills. While you spend months on end writing your little stories –

he's on his feet, pacing the kitchen floor –

and hoping your agent can finagle an advance or you're waiting on royalties to roll in…IF they roll in…the mortgage still has to be paid. The electric bill. The water bill. Gas for the car. Dog food for Gidget. The money has to come from somewhere. Guess where that somewhere is.

Ok, Ok. I understand. Look, let's not turn on each other and just try and figure out how we can get around Dirk's edict from on high. You need to be able to fly. I need to get off island to meet with my publisher. We both have to do these things in order to earn our living. There's got to be a way we can disobey a direct order. The look on Marc's face tells me he's suspicious of what I'm suggesting.

I am wounded beyond my ability to express. My "little" stories? Finagle an advance? IF royalties come in? WOW! What am I supposed to do with that? But he's right. Living requires cash flow. My cash flow is not predictable and it's tenuous. When, my first novel sold, it was a hit, especially locally…not just on Tybee but throughout Georgia. It dropped in April just in time for the spring break, vacation season to start and it was a local phenomenon. Lots of good press and a good review or two from a couple of high profile mystery novelists and I made a meaningful amount of money, which to our credit we saved most of but spent some to pay off our car loans and settle other debts. But, that only lasted for so long. My second book was not such a success, less cash flowing in and a little less confidence from my publisher. Maybe I was a one hit wonder.

I'd have been in good company with Margaret Mitchel and Syliva Plath. They and other one hit wonders only had one really good book in them. But, good company doesn't pay the bills. I've soldiered on and my third book in the Tybee Island mystery series fell flat. Sales made back the cash advance my publisher gave me, but little more. So, now their confidence in me has definitely waned and Marc and I are living frugally and it's his teaching daredevils to fly and letting crazy tourists sky dive from his Cessna that is paying the day-to-day bills.

And, I absolutely HATE! It. I've always been somewhat independent and been able to pretty much make my own way in the world. For my entire first career in the investment business, I'd dreamed of being a mystery writer and making my living as a published author. Hard, stressful days were managed by thoughts of sitting on a beach with my computer and crafting a rousing good yarn about murder and mayhem. And, a couple of years ago – after my first husband died - I took my savings and decided to live off of it for one year while I wrote my first book. One last chance and a risky investment in myself and my dream. And, as I said, at first I enjoyed some publishing and financial success. But, not all I've touched has turned to gold.

So, Marc and I are working as a team to make our lives a success, by our own standards of happiness and security. But, I absolutely cannot loose my publisher or my agent and we can't afford for Marc not to be able to fly and earn a living. So, what – indeed – can we do to get ourselves freed of this on island restriction, so we can resume our livelihoods.

I wonder. Please dear God, open a path for us.

CHAPTER 7

It's a quiet, sunny Sunday morning. A nice respite from the literal and figurative storm of the past couple of days. Michael has weakened to a rainstorm and moved on out into the Atlantic, leaving Tybee sunny and feeling washed clean. Marc and I slept in after all the excitement and sleeplessness of Friday night and Saturday morning and our argument from yesterday has passed like the storm.

But, I'm up now, Gidget has been fed and walked and she's settled at my feet while I am sitting at the kitchen table working on my current 'little story" – and yes I'm still wounded by that comment – when all of a sudden I hear a faint buzzing sound off somewhere distant in the house. It catches my subconscious attention but Gidget's head has popped up. She knows exactly what it is and she emphatically does not like it.

The buzzing sound is getting louder as I sit here and try to concentrate. Which is hard enough being distracted by the events of Saturday morning and trying to pull together the threads of a new story, under the pressure of my most recent flop and the scathing, shouting tirade I received from my agent over having to cancel my meeting with my publisher. So, my mind is all a jumble and I'm trying to concentrate and create and out of the corner of my eye comes this little yellow buzzing thing, tiny, just three inches in diagonal length and four ounces in weight, making like a hummingbird toward me. I don't flinch or duck. It's just Marc flying a tiny drone, using the house as his make shift obstacle course. Now that he's grounded, he's got a flying itch he desperately needs to scratch...so I'm OK with this.

Marc was in the Air Force and spent part of his military career flying drones and doing some secret snoopy snoop doggie dog kinda stuff which he has never and will never tell me or anyone about. I think it might've had something to do with the first Gulf War and the Iranian border. Or maybe he was just messing with the Russians, flicking the Kremlin lights on and off. He still has to maintain his secret security clearance and I've heard from one of his old military commanders that his retirement file is coded RED (retired extremely dangerous). After his military service, Marc blasted off to Alaska where he spent a couple of years as a bush pilot in Unakalete, returning to his home in New York to fly cargo planes for FedEx. The later stages of his flying career he spent flying Lear Jets for an international medical evacuation company headquartered in Georgia, which is where he met me and the second love of his life, Tybee Island. Sometimes, I jokingly call Tybee his mistress and for some reason it annoys him. But, I don't mind if she is one of his top five true loves. I love her too. And, as I've mentioned, I am truly content to live out my days with the two of them.

But, right now, I'm pausing my writing to stop and look this little yellow buzzing annoyance in its tiny camera eye. I stick out my tongue.

Marc is watching and he waggles the little thing at me to say "HI". Marc and I have been restricted to Tybee and not allowed off island by our beloved Sheriff, Dirk Bentley, and that means Marc cannot fly. So, not only is he not making his living teaching others to fly or taking the crazies sky diving, it also means he is bored out of his scull and can only satisfy his insatiable desire to fly by annoying me with his ever expanding collection of drones.

For the gazillionth time I think to myself how lucky Marc is to have a woman in his life who not only is patient but isn't even that bothered by being buzzed by a drone inside her own kitchen. It's a good thing one of us is easy going.

I try to shoo the drone away when it suddenly occurs to me that maybe there is some practical application for Marc's pent up energy and flying skills.

Marc and I decided that the only real way we can both get out from under the "on island" restriction is if we can find out the who and maybe the why of Joe's death. Once the case is solved and closed, then we can resume our normal lives. If we can do it quickly, maybe I can make my meeting in New York with my publisher after all – save what tatters remain of my writing career – and Marc can resume his flying with minimal disruption to our cash flow.

In order to accomplish this, we need more information than we already have and I'm thinking the place to start is back where Joe's body was found, see if there's any sign of a struggle, patterns in the sea oats, something – anything – missed by the Sheriff's department.

Even if the area around where Joe's body was found wasn't cordoned off, it's actually illegal in Georgia to walk in the dunes where the sea oats grow. They are a protected plant species, vital to preserving the sandy beaches and preventing erosion. The oats are the threads that hold the shoreline's fabric together.

And, it's still October and the loggerhead nesting season doesn't officially end till the end of the month. The last nest dug and the last clutch of eggs laid was just over 90 days ago, so baby turtles are still hatching and digging their way to the surface. And, again, it is illegal in Georgia to even go near these babies, let alone disturb or touch them in any way.

So, I'm thinking maybe Marc and I could walk a little ways down the beach from our home (which is closer to the north end of the island) and he could use one of his drones to fly low and slow over the area where Joe's body was found and we could get a really good look around. Marc tells me it can go slow, hover, won't just drop out of the sky, and the camera can send video and pictures back to a computer that we can record and review later. We'll have to be strategic about the ground we cover because Marc says the battery life on the little baby drone is only about 10 minutes. But 10 minutes of snoopy snoop doggie dogging should be plenty.

The drone is still buzzing around the kitchen. Gidget has moved up under the table and has her head laying on my feet. She does not like these drones for what reason I don't know and she's never said. I dane to disturb her as I get up and grab a piece of paper and a marker and write a note to Marc, holding it up I front of the drone's eye. It says:

Watson, come here I need you.

CHAPTER 8

Marc has recharged the baby drone's battery and about half an hour later we are leaving the house, this time with Gidget in tow. I have her on a leash this morning, just in case there's a little sand crab or baby turtle that catches her fancy and she decides to run off on her own. Great Pyrenees are highly intelligent, a little stubborn and will make up their own minds about what they will and won't do. So, it's easier for me if she's on a leash at my side. A restriction of freedom that she has made quite clear she is not happy about.

I grab my straw bag, into which Marc has deposited the baby drone, it's control box and his ipad, which will receive the video transmission from our little yellow spy. The three of us walk out the front door (which we do not lock behind us) of our story and a half, blue and white cape cod cottage, down the sandy front walk, through the white picket fence gate and make a left down the ancient cracked concrete sidewalk toward the end of our cul de sac that breaks onto the beach. To anyone passing by, we look like just a nice middle-aged couple and their dog out for a Sunday morning walk on the beach. But, really we are two super sleuths and one talking dog out to start gathering clues to solve a murder and get the train of our lives and our livelihoods back on track.

Once on the beach we head north along the water line, Gidget walking ahead of us at the full outstreatched length of her leash, looking back occasionally to make sure we are walking as fast as we can. She likes being on the beach and getting her little princess toes wet in the surf. She does not like the dry part of the beach because the sand blows around and gets all matted in her long white hair and makes her itchy. So, she stays on the wet, hard packed sand and along the water's edge.

About a half mile on, I can see the yellow police tape and we're getting close to the location where Joe's body was found. As we approach the beach area in front of the cordoned off area, Gidget stops and sticks her nose flat on the sand and I can see little puffs of sand grains jumping in the air as she's sniffing and snorting. Her tail is curled high over her back, indicating a heightened state of alert. I go to her, nudge her head aside and say:

Let me see, girl. Whatcha got there?

And sure enough she's spotted something round and shiny pushed in the sand. I dig my finger around it and pull out a brass 9mm shell casing.

Hey Marc, look at this.

He comes over and takes the shell casing from me, turning it over in his fingers.

Huh…that's interesting. Six feet right in front of where Joe's body was found. Funny the deputies didn't find this.

Well, it was pushed down in the sand and Gidget just nosed it out. Maybe they just didn't see it when they were here in the pitch dark on Saturday morning. I doubt they were combing the beach with a metal detector looking for bullet shell casings when it looked like the cause of death was that fence post.

Yeah. Maybe. We'll drop this off at Dirk's office later. You still need to let Lucy take down your statement from Saturday anyway.

Marc stuffs the shell casing in his pants pocket. No sense treating it like evidence now with a potential fingerprint, since we've both handled it and Gidget put her nose all over it.

Marc takes my straw bag and fishes out the baby drone. He sets it on the hard pack sand and turns on the radio control box. I've got the ipad out, turned on and the video app open and ready to receive the drone's feed. Marc starts its little motor and when the buzzing starts Gidget – who was looking farther down the beach and not watching Marc – is startled and jumps a foot off the ground and growls:

Shit

Huh? What'd you say?

Um…sorry, I just sneezed.

I thought you said, Shit.

No, just a sneeze. A little sand in my nose.

Oh. Well, Ok. Godzilla.

Thank you. I give Gidget a sideways look of caution and I swear she shrugs her shoulders. One of these days, I'm going to have to make her tell me why the buzzing sound of these drones is so frightening to her. But, for now, I just walk up close to her and put my hand on her head and pull her close to my leg.

The little drone slowly lifts into the air and Marc sends it in the direction of the taped off area. It flies slowly at first and then picks up a little speed. The sea oats are tall and blowing in the wind, so Marc has to maneuver it to avoid getting it's propellers tangled in the feathery panicles. But, our little yellow spy deftly wends and winds its way into the dune to where there is still a churned sea of sand and destroyed plants where Joe's body had lain.

Slowly, Marc guides the drone over the length of the body depression and turns it so its camera is basically panning left to right, searching for anything at all that might be of interest.

He has programmed the tiny camera with its even tinier computer chip to link wirelessly to his ipad and I'm watching the images on the screen as he slowly maneuvers around the site. As the drone flies lower to the ground, I can see sand being poofed into the air and in a flash I think I see something black just under the surface skin of the ground.

Marc, hold it. Go back.

What?

Fly backwards a little. I think I see something. The drone was blowing around some sand and I think I saw something black just…there… no, no, go backwards about an inch more. Yep, right there. Can you hold it stable there and come look at this picture.

Marc gingerly makes his way over to me and rapidly glances at the ipad screen and sure enough, the propellers are blowing sand around and uncovering something black, looking for all the world like the but end of a pistol grip.

Well, damn. Look at that.

What do we do? Should we sneak over and dig it up.

No, let's take the shell casing over to Dirk's office and show him this video and let one of his deputies come dig up whatever it is. Here, let me get the drone back, you hit save on that file.

Marc walks back over to where he can more clearly see the drone and orders it to return, and like a falcon returning to its master, it promptly buzzes back to Marc and land's slick and snot right at his feet. It's those sexy pilot's hands at work.

OK, then. Let's get back to the house, brush off and get down to the sheriff's office.

We repack the drone and the controller into my straw bag. Marc takes the ipad from me and makes sure the file is saved before he folds it away and drops it into my bag. Gidget leads us at a slow gallop as we walk as fast as we can in the shifting sand back down the beach toward our house. My calf muscles are screaming by the time we exit the beach and climb back on to the solid street and sidewalk.

Once we're back at the house, I turn on the garden hose I've left coiled in the front flower bed and I give us all a quick rinse off and we dry our feet with an old towel I've brought.

We're entering the house, Marc going first to open the door when I hear

Ugh

and the deep, shuddering thud as his body hits the floor in the front hall. I look up from watching my feet climb the front stoop to see a tall figure, dressed in faded jeans, a white t-shirt and a blue bandana covering his face fling wide the door and lunge at me. As he's grabbing for my shoulders, Gidget lunges from beside me, landing all 100 pounds of her weight onto his chest with her front paws, knocking him backward so that he falls right on top of Marc's body and she immediately opens wide her jaws to latch onto the intruder's neck.

This is what Great Pyrenees do. They are recklessly brave in the protection of their families and they have been known to attack bears and kill wolves with the sudden decisive move of going for the throat.

Whoever our attacker is would be spouting arterial blood and bleeding out right now if it weren't for the fact that Gidget doesn't have any teeth. As a bate dog in her dog fighting days, the demons who owned her broke out all her front teeth and canines so she couldn't fight back and injure the more valuable fighting dogs. When she was rescued, one thing Marc and I did was take her to a vet dental specialist whose only option was to remove the remnants of all her front teeth and canines. So, this punk's life was saved by Gidget only being able to gum his carotids. But, her powerful jaws and body combined with her weight had him well under her control.

In the meantime, I'm screaming my head off, which catches the attention of my neighbor, Tim, who is working in this front yard with his wife, Cheryl. Tim was once a Marine, and - you know what they say - always a Marine. He comes running, assesses the situation, drops back into his combat training and pushes me aside, grabs Gidget by the collar and wrenches her off the attacker, grabs him by his shoulders and – literally – picks him up off the ground and body slams him onto our front porch, banging his head with a satisfying THUNK! on the metal porch railing.

Tim, breathless, turns to me and asks if I'm OK, which I am, but Marc is moaning as he's beginning to regain consciousness. Gidget and I run to him and while I'm trying to help him sit up, Gidget begins whimpering and kissing his face, desperately sniffing to inspect the injured spot on his noggin. I touch it gingerly with my fingertips as Marc winces and yells

Ow!

And I can feel there's already a nice little goose egg forming on his head.

Cheryl must've pulled out her cell phone and called 911 because within what seems like only seconds, Sheriff Bentley and two cruisers come roaring down our quiet little lane, sirens blaring, tires squealing. As they jump out of their cars, I yell for someone to call an ambulance. Dirk runs up to me and says,

Already rolling. Stay down, Marc. Don't get up.

Now, there's three of us trying to touch Marc's head as he desperately tries to push our probing hands and fingers away. He doesn't try to push Gidget away. He let's her sit close to him and minister to his pains, remaining on the ground as commanded.

A few minutes later, the ambulance arrives, with paramedics jumping into action. I look up into the shocked eyes of Marc's son, Tyler, who is a paramedic with the Tybee Island Fire and Rescue and one of the first responders to our emergency.

Dad, are you OK? Oh My God! What happened?

Tyler looks from his dad to me back to his dad, waiting for an explanation.

I'm fine, son. Go see about that man on the porch. I'm fine!

By now we know it's a man because one of Dirk's deputies immediately unmasked him when they arrived in an effort to see if he was OK. A second ambulance is roaring up to a halt in front of our house. I know it's for the attacker but, frankly, I couldn't care less. I'm too focused on Marc.

I start blathering to Dirk about how we were just coming back from running the drone over the beach where Joe's body was found and how Marc had just opened the door when this guy jumped us.

You were coming back from WHAT?!

Uh oh.

Ummm. A walk on the beach?

No ma'am. Please tell me you did not just say what I think you just said.

Ummm. Ok.

Gidget who is understanding every word being said, still keyed up from saving her master's life and sensing the heat of Dirk's rising anger, has walked over to me and positioned herself between me and the Sheriff. She has actually backed her backside between my legs, her head and grimacing, toothless muzzle facing Dirk. I hear her low warning growl and I put my hand on her back and say,

Ok, Gidgie. It's OK. Dirk you might want to back up a few feet and calm down a little. Gidget's not having any of this. Please just let me explain after we get Marc to the hospital.

I'm not going to the hospital. I'm fine.

You most certainly are not fine. You just had a nasty knock on your head that left you unconscious. Tyler, tell your Dad he has to go to the hospital.

Dad, you have to go to the hospital.

As he's saying this, Tyler and his co-medic each grab one of Marc's arms and hoist him up onto a stretcher. And, as Marc makes to protest being kidnapped against his will, spouting off about how he has lived on this planet for more than half a century and served in the military for twenty god damn years and has had nastier knocks than this and (blah blah blah) the two brawny young men, strap him down and wheel him toward the ambulance.

Yeah, Yeah, Yeah. I hear ya, Dad. You're going to the hospital, period!

Tyler climbs into the back of the ambulance as the stretcher bearing Marc is lifted and banged into the back, the doors slammed and locked. I see Marc through the back windows, straining to sit up, both his middle fingers raised in defiance as the driver runs to get in the front, puts the truck in gear and speeds off, sirens blaring.

Oh, God. I'm going to have to hear about this from now until death do us part. Marc is very head strong and views pain as just weakness leaving the body. Hospital's are for sissies, which he most certainly is NOT!

But, still, at least Marc is off to the hospital with his son, who I know will watch over him whether he wants it or not, leaving me available to continue to explain ourselves to our Sheriff.

CHAPTER 9

Here.

Dirk pulls a chair back from in front of his desk and motions for me to sit. He moves his giant bulk around to the other side of his desk and sits heavily in his chair, leaning back and watching me. We've arrived back at the Sheriff's office and now it's time for the fat lady to sing.

Let me just call Anne real quick.

I need to tell her what's happened. I know she'll want to rush over to the Tybee Island Emergency Care, which is the closest thing to an actual emergency room on the island. The nearest hospital is in Savannah, 17 miles away. There's nothing the hospital can do that this well equipped emergency care facility can't do, so this is where Tyler will take his father and where Marc will receive expert care.

Dirk waits patiently as I finish my call with Anne, reassuring her that her dad will be OK and that Tyler is with him. She should go to the Emergi-care place if she wants to but be prepared for his ill temper and under no circumstances is she to let him bully her into breaking him out of there.

He has to stay until the doctor says he's OK to leave and come home.

She understands. She's not easily intimidated by anyone and she will call me if there's any development I need to know about. So, satisfied Marc is in the best of hands, I now need to focus on the task at hand…

…Explaining to the Sheriff what Marc and I were doing on the beach earlier today.

As I tuck my phone in my back pocket, I move to sit in the chair proffered, Gidget staying close to me. I ask her to sit and she politely complies. But, her eyes are glued on Dirk. She's still not happy about his demonstrated anger toward me back at the house.

Well, as long as I'm here do you want me to give Lucy my statement from Saturday morning?

I ask sheepishly, trying to pivot by striking a helpful tone that I hope will diffuse some of his clear and present irritation with me.

LUCY! Dirk yells. In comes Lucy. She's the officer who manages the administrative side of the department. Essentially, an office manager, secretary, organizational maven, IT specialist, paperwork whiz and file clerk. Meaning, she's really in charge around here and everyone knows it.

She's a truly stunning, 40-something widow with thick flaming red hair, brilliant green eyes and non-stop curves and boobs. Even my loyal, loving Marc can't help but watch her every move when she enters a room. She's also the sweetest natured, most capable and intelligent woman I've met in a long time and I adore her. I count her among my girl posse, along with Marc's daughter Anne, The Sisters and Gidget, of course.

You bellowed, Master?

Lucy, would you mind taking down Miss Amy's statement. She's just about to tell me what she and Marc were up to this morning down on the beach, contaminating our crime scene and interfering with a police investigation.

Now, Sheriff.

Now, Amy. Listen to me right now.

No, Dirk! I have to tell you something and I need you to listen to me right now.

WHAT?! DAMN IT!

Ok. While we were walking on the beach, Gidget found a 9mm shell casing pushed down in the sand, about 6 feet right in front of where Joe's body was found.

What! Where is it?

Well, it's in Marc's jeans pants pocket. Gidget found it, I dug it out, gave it to Marc and he put it in his pants. So, someone needs to call over to the Emergi-care place and have them get that out of his pants and save it for you. We were going to bring it here to you this afternoon, until we got way laid back at the house.

Also, Marc flew one of his drones over the place where the body was and we've recorded some footage that we think shows there might be something buried a few feet from where his body was. It's black. The video is in a file saved on Marc's ipad. The ipad was in my straw bag along with the drone equipment. But, I don't know what happened to my bag. It must still be at the house, maybe on the front porch. So, someone needs to go back to our house and retrieve my bag and bring it here.

OK. OK. Hold on. So, you and Marc found a 9mm shell casing in the sand and you recorded video footage from a drone that shows something is buried near where Joe's body was laying.

Yes. But, someone has got to go right now and get that shell casing out of Marc's pants and get my bag with the ipad in it before these things disappear.

Lucy?

On it.

Like I said, Lucy is the one who is really in charge around here. She's the one who knows how to make things happen.

Ok, now Missy. Let's just take a deep breath. Lucy'll get a deputy to retrieve these things and bring them here to me. Between now and then, tell me what in the name of holy CSI were you and Marc doing flying a drone around out there.

Well, listen, you've put us on what is essentially island arrest. I can't go meet with my publisher and Marc can't fly. Neither of us can make our living under these conditions. We needed to do something to try and figure this thing out.

Riddle me this bat girl, what exactly do you think I and my deputies have been trying to do for the past couple of days?

Crickets.

Ah, see now he's made a good point. I hate it when he makes a good point. I guess Marc and I had gotten so caught up in thinking about our own predicament and what we could do to bring about a quick resolution to benefit ourselves that we sort of forgot there was a highly trained police force already looking into things.

Weeelll....

Yeah. Well, thanks for the vote of confidence, Amy. If you'll recall, the last time you got yourself mixed up in something nefarious, it was I...not you or Marc...but I...who determined who the killer was and it was I who realized you had not just disappeared but had been abducted and it was I who bird dogged you and saved your little lady butt. Remember...?

Ummm...yes. I say sheepishly, using my most appeasing little girl voice.

It's true. Sheriff Bentley had "officially" solved the case of my murdered friend, Lisa, and had literally saved my life with one expert sniper shot right between the eyes of the killer. A killer who at that precise moment had held me in a death grip choke hold with a very large and scary knife at my throat.

And, by the way, Missy. Let me just inform you that in the last 24 hours, we have not just been resting on our laurels, hanging out at Huca poo's and wandering the beach.

Ouch...

The county coroner has already examined the body, removed the four by four fence posting, run an MRI scan on Joe's head and found some indication that a bullet was fired into his scull at pretty close range and that it was this bullet wound that was the actual cause of death. Apparently, the fence post was jammed in his head afterward to try and mask the bullet wound. So, it would appear, we have a premeditated crime. It's not for sure the bullet fired into his brain was premeditated but clearly there was some thought put into trying to cover it up afterward.

Wow, now that's progress.

What does it mean, "found some indication"?

Well, found an actual bullet in his scull.

Oh...

Ah, yeah that would be an indication all right. So, now all you have to do is find out who shot Joe in the head and figure out if it is the same person who jammed the post in his head to obfuscate the bullet wound.

Uh…yeah…that's right.

So, that shell casing and what we think might be a gun buried in the sand could be just the clues you need to solidify your theory of the crime and maybe even identify the killer.

Uh…yeah…maybe.

Wow, so Marc and I have helped you then, huh? Not contaminated anything but actually furthered your investigation.

I hear Gidget give a little snort of satisfaction and I know she's thinking – but not saying – something like…

so there…

Uh…no, now wait just a minute there. I do not need your help with this investigation. In fact, if you continue to involve yourself in it, I might have to arrest you for interfering in an active investigation.

But, Dirk…

No butts, no nuts, no coconuts, Missy.

I'm laughing now and so is he. Dirk really does like me and Marc and I think he thinks of us as his friends. We certainly respect and trust him. He is an honorable man with a strong sense of right and wrong and devotion to duty. And, since he saved my life that time, Marc and I owe him a debt of loyalty we can never repay. So now that he's ordered us to butt out of his investigation, I suppose we'll have to, actually, butt out.

Listen, Amy, Lucy won't be back for a while so why don't you just go on over to the emerge-care place and check on Marc. I'll catch up with you guys later today after we get that shell casing and the video and get them logged into evidence. I want to get that shell casing and whatever is under the sand over to the crime lab in Savannah so they can be checked for fingerprints. You're right about one thing, these may be the leads we need to identify the killer.

Well I can tell you there won't be any fingerprints on the shell casing. Other than mine and Marc's and maybe a nose print from Gidget. We handled it pretty extensively digging it out of the sand.

Be that as it may. Go on now, go see about Marc.

Since this is exactly what I am anxious to do, I take him up on his offer to catch me later. After Marc and his attacker were taken to the hospital, Dirk had allowed me to drive myself over to his office. So, I've got my jeep parked out front.

I open the door for Gidget and she trots out ahead of me and runs to the Jeep and jumps in the front driver's seat, sitting there panting a little and smiling as she watches me walk across the parking lot.

Uh Uh. Move over. I make a hand motion to shoo her over to the passenger seat and she grunts a little disappointment. I jump into the driver's seat, reach over and pull the seat belt around her and buckle her in and fire up the engine. Just as Marc's motor glider is his baby, my yellow Jeep Wrangler is my baby and I'm so relieved and happy she started right up for me this time. Marc thinks she's a POS, and when he starts in on how I need to get rid of her, I start referring to his German-made glider as fraulein. We know how to push each other's buttons.

But, today the Jeep is purring like a kitten and I make it over to the emergi-care in about 10 minutes. I can't believe there's a parking place right in front and I swing into the spot. I release Gidget's seat belt buckle and we both jump out and head for the front door. As we're walking into reception, I see Anne coming down the hall and as we meet, I embrace her in a warm hug that only a mother can give. Anne, is a grown woman with her own biological mother, but I absolutely adore her and I'd have been so happy if I could've been her mother. I'm careful not to try and act too motherly or tell her what to do. But, whenever I see her I can't help but wrap my arms around her, pull her close and hold her tight.

I release her from my mama bear hug and I see she's been crying.

Oh, God. What did he say?

He can be so mean when he's being restrained.

I know honey. I told you he'd be fit to be tied and I'm guessing that's what's happened, huh? Did he try to escape?

Yes.

She snuffles her runny nose and I use my thumb to wipe a wet eye.

And Tyler and one of the doctors had to hold him down and sedate him to get him to lie down and be quiet.

Uh huh. Where is he?

Just down the hall in room 5.

I glance down the hall and I can see one of Sherriff Bentley's deputies standing guard at the door of a nearby room. Now it dawns on me that the man who attacked us must be in this same facility in a room on the same hall with Marc. It's a somewhat small place and my neighbor Tim did thump on him pretty hard when he came to our rescue. So, of course he'd have had to be taken for medical care just like Marc. But, it still strikes me as odd to think he's close by to Marc. But the deputy is there and he's big and scary and armed. So, I'm not really worried that somehow the wounded idiot is going to try and finish the job.

I put my arm around Anne's shoulder and we walk down the hall toward room 5 where Marc is. As we pass by this other room, I look up at the deputy, who knows me and I say,

Hey, Michael.

Hey there, Miss Amy.

Michael Matthews is a strange combination of warrior and peace-maker. He is one of Sheriff Bentley's most capable deputies, a very large, muscular, imposing, armed African American man in his mid-thirties. Highly trained, intelligent, and lethal when he needs to be. But, he is also gentle and caring and very concerned about the environment. He was born and raised on Tybee and loves the Island as much or more than anyone. He's also very involved with the Island's volunteer group that assists the Georgia Department of Natural Resources in protecting it as part of our national shoreline. Turtles, particularly the baby turtles, newly hatched and struggling to the sea, are his most ardent passion and he's been known to camp out on the beach for days on end during the nesting season, protecting the loggerhead turtles at their most vulnerable.

In addition to shrimp trawling, pollution and land development in nesting areas, loggerhead sea turtles have become an endangered species because of illegal poaching. They've been captured and killed in brutal ways for their meat and eggs and shells and in some parts of the world, the eggs are considered an aphrodisiac delicacy, believed to enhance male performance. Slicing open the pregnant momma turtles and eating their eggs right out of their bellies while the turtles are still alive is only one of the heinous fates that awaits these gentle creatures. A pregnant momma turtle can fetch a king's ransom on the black market.

But someone would have to be pretty desperate to try this on Tybee with Deputy Matthews standing guard over the momma turtles digging their nests and the baby turtles when they are hatching. I believe he would in fact not hesitate to shoot to kill if he caught someone trying to hurt one of his turtles or their babies.

I look up into his eyes and I pull my sweetest smile from deep inside my heart and I ask him:

Is that guy in there? The one who attacked Marc?

Yes, Ma'am. But don't worry. He ain't goin' no where.

Oh, Micheal. I know. You'd never let him outta that room. I'm not worried. I'm still smiling into his eyes and in that moment, he locks eyes with me and breaks a small smile and I can feel the little energy jolt inside my body as I connect with him. So, while I have him under my spell, I ask:

So, could I maybe just look in at him? I never did get to see his face and I'd like to know who did this to us. And why.

Of course, he's supposed to say "NO! absolutely not!" . But, again, I have him under my spell and I can feel happiness radiating off of him. It's the little piece of Joy I sent to him when we looked into each others eyes and I smiled at him from my heart. It's a physical sensation that I have the ability to push out of myself and give to someone. It's like the sound of a distant bell tinkling so softly it tickles the inside of your gut and makes you want to giggle.

I've used this gift many times in my life to make friends and influence people. It's the reason I knew Micki and Louise Huca poo also had "the gift" the very first time I met them and why their business is so incredibly successful and everyone is drawn there. Joy is ancient and powerful magic, second only to the most powerful magic of all, Love.

When Jesus died on the cross as the ultimate and final sacrifice to redeem all of humanity back to a Holy God, the absolute, unbreakable, irresistible power of Love and Joy was sealed forever. And by their very nature, can never be used for ill will or harm.

There's way too much hurt and pain in this world and people who have been hurt the most in their lives are irresistibly drawn to people like me and the Sisters. So, Michael can't help himself and he says:

Sure

As he moves to open the door for me. I tell Anne to wait with Gidgie and the deputy and I step into the room with the man who could've killed Marc and destroyed my life.

I find the person who attacked us lying in a hospital bed in one of those gowns that are way to big and revealing. He's a very thin young man, half conscious from the thumping he took from my Marine neighbor friend, Tim, and probably from a bunch of meds the hospital has given him. He doesn't seem so scary right now and I find that what I feel is anger mixed with pity. Not sure why I feel sorry for him since he was the one who violated our home and proceeded to attack us. On Tybee, we all leave our doors unlocked with the unbreakable implicit agreement between us all that we respect each other's property, privacy and person. You do not – I repeat – you do NOT breach the sanctity of the threshold of another person's home without being invited. And, you certainly do not do them any harm. It's the rule of living on a small island and being apart of a community of people who genuinely care for each other. You give respect, you get respect. It's that simple!

But, lying here in this hospital bed is a young man, frail and kinda sad looking. His cheeks are suken and his pale skin has the acne and palor of someone who is a habitual drug user. He, clearly, is not healthy and is being slowly ravaged by his addiction. So, I decide to ignore my anger and when he opens his frightened eyes and looks at me, I return a steady gaze directly into his green eyes and I speak to him in a kind, soft voice that lets him know I am not here to harm him.

When he speaks, I am surprised by his manners and seeming sincerity.

My name is Jesse Blankenship and I am mighty sorry for hurtin' you and yours, ma' am.

I've never been in a situation like this before and I'm not really sure what to do or say. My goal is to get information, specifically, why did he break into hour home and why did he try to attack us when he was leaving. Why not just sneak out the back and hope no one saw him?

Jesse, my name is Amy and I appreciate your apology. Marc is the name of the man you attacked and could've potentially killed if it hadn't been for our dog stopping you.

Yes, ma' am. That's one brave, scary dog you got there.

Yeah, you really have no idea how lucky you are you're even alive right now. She went for your throat and if she could've, should've killed you outright in Marc's defense. In fact, I brought her here with me to guard Marc, in addition to Sheriff Bentley's deputies. And, if she even gets a whiff of you anywhere near Marc, you're a dead man. For your sake, I hope you understand what I am telling you.

Yes, Ma' am.

In fact, she's sitting outside your door right now and what I'm hoping is going to happen in the next two minutes is you are going to tell me the absolute truth – in detail – as to why you did what you did.

Jesse's eyes widen at the news that Gidget is only just feet away. And, he begins to tell me what he thinks I want to know.

Ma' am, please. I ain't never done nothin like this before. I was only just looking for somethin' and if you hadn't come home when you did, I'd have left your house and you'd probly never even knowd I'd been there.

He pauses.

And…

And what?

And what were you looking for?

Well, I saw you out on the beach early Saturday morning. I was there to get some stuff from Joe. I don't know if you know this, but his brother, Rodney takes some pretty heavy duty meds and I got some friends and myself who like 'em too. And, Joe gets some of Rodney's pills and sells 'em to me. He aint cheap, but he's the only one on this whole island who can get his hands on beckys and oxies. But, my friends'll pay just about any price to get their shit. So, I was there to do a deal, that's all. It was still pretty windy from the storm, but the rain had stopped and it was so late, I just sat down right there in the weeds, watin' for Joe. I heard him come walking up, whistling low and talkin' to hisself. Something about some damn bitch he screwed once and now he was gonna screw her again. I was just about to call his name, when I heard this loud bang. Just one. Like I said, it was still real windy from the storm but I could tell it was a gun shot. I heard enough of that in my life. So, I just sat there real still like, trying not to make a sound. I heard a woman's voice but couldn't quite make out what she was sayin'. I waited a while, not sure how long. When, I did finally get the courage to move I sat up on my knees and looked and saw Joe's body lying on the ground and you standing near Joe's feet. You was carryin' a big bag, pulled out your phone and made a call and a few minutes later, the Sheriff and all his deputies showed up. So, I just stayed put and waited to see what was happening.

Later, it seemed to me that maybe you'd shot Joe and maybe you took his stash. So, after you left, I followed you back down the beach to your house and decided I'd come back later and see if I could find 'em. I got bills to pay and friends still lookin' to score. So, I just found me a place across the street to lay low and watched your house for a while and the next day I saw you and your man and your dog leave and walk off toward the beach. I thought you'd be gone a while and I'd have a chance to search your house. I didn't think you'd have come back so soon or your dog would be so vicious. You guys took me by surprise and I was just trying to get the hell outta there.

Please, Ma'am, you gotta believe me. I ain't never done nothing violent in my whole life. I ain't never even held a gun or beat up nobody. I take some pills sometimes, but that's it. And, I was scared, thinking you'd already maybe killed one person. So, I just started swingin and trying to run.

I don't know why, but I totally believed his story. Like the Sisters, I have the gift and I can always – always – tell when someone is lying. And when someone is telling the truth, I can feel its presence just like a person is standing next to me.

OK, listen, Jesse. I believe you. And, I appreciate you telling me what happened. I cannot forgive what you did but I figure you'll pay for it one way or another and it's not up to me to wish you ill. The best thing you can do for yourself is to tell Sheriff Bentley exactly what you just told me, drug deals and all. And, if you cooperate with him, you'll find he will be fair with you. In your situation, that's the best you can hope for. If Marc comes out of this unharmed and I hear from the Sheriff that you've been completely honest and helpful in his investigation into Joe Smith's murder, I will tell him I believe your story and that maybe the best thing for you might not be jail but some sort of rehab or probation and community service. But, Marc and I are your victims. Don't ever forget that. We'd be perfectly justified to ask for revenge as justice for what you did to Marc. But, if you help the Sheriff, we might help you. Understand?

Yes, Ma' am. I understand.

CHAPTER 10

I am sitting in Marc's room, next to his bed, holding his hand, which is ice cold. Marc has been sedated (probably to keep him from escaping the hospital before the doctor actually discharges him) and he's sleeping and snoring slightly. When Gidget followed me into his room, she gasped at the sight of him and immediately went and jumped up into his bed, stretched out her full length along his side and gently laid her head across his chest. I plan to let Gidget stay here with Marc overnight, knowing she would give her life to protect him.

Just like Jesse, Marc's room is guarded by one of the Sheriff's deputies. Another very large, scary man who knows us well and I don't need to cast a spell over him to get him to let me and Anne and Gidgie in to see Marc.

The TV mounted on the ceiling is on, volume low and I glance up at it and see the mid day news cast is replaying a press conference held earlier in the morning by the Sheriff. He must've called this impromptu press conference shortly after I'd left his office. I reach for the bedside control and try to figure out the button for the TV volume without accidentally calling the nurse. Dirk rarely speaks to the media – he has a "media person" for that – and I've never seen him actually speaking on camera before.

Thank you all for coming this morning. As Prosecutor Stone mentioned, we're here to talk about the death of Mr. Joe Smith. Before we get started on that, I do want to acknowledge two people who have worked extraordinarily hard on this case. Deputy Sheriff Michael Mathews and agent Ellsworth Druthers pathologist with the Georgia Criminal Investigations Bureau. I've brought them here this morning because we work for the public and 1 want all our "bosses" to know that this is a team effort. There's no one person who does everything in relation to an investigation like this. There are many hands on deck and officers who dedicate themselves to bringing justice to the families and victims of crimes. They've been working many long hours every day and late into the night every night since Mr. Smith's body was found on the north beach.

I understand and appreciate the public's concern over the events of last Saturday morning. We so rarely have any violent crime on the island and for the most part we all live peacefully together as a tight knit community. So, it's understandable that there would be an inordinate amount of worry and concern over the events of the past few days. The County Prosecutor and I thought it would be a good idea to allay some of those concerns and put to rest some rumors that have been floating around by holding this very unusual press conference.

During this investigation, we have discovered that what was originally presenting as a storm related accident was in fact a homicide and we believe we are now looking for more than one person in the commission and the cover up of this crime. While a final determination of the time of death is still pending, the autopsy of Mr. Smith has revealed the actual cause of death was a gun shot wound to the head and not the impalement of a fence post. And we now believe the evidence shows the fence post originally found lodged in Mr. Smith's head was placed there in order to obfuscate the bullet wound. As a result, the death of Mr. Smith has been determined to be a homicide and not an accident.

Further investigation has led us to discover a 9mm pistol in close proximity to Mr. Smith's body and upon further examination of the weapon we have developed two persons of interest we will be bringing in for questioning and are looking for a third person of interest.

As I'm sitting here watching this press conference and thinking how fortunate we are Marc was not injured more than he was, the door swings open and in walks a doctor, followed close on by Sherriff Bentley. The doctor greets me with:

Ma'am.

Gidget raises her head from Marc's chest to see who has come into his room. She'll decide for herself if this is something to be concerned about. She plops her head back across his chest. Apparently, she's decided it's not worthy of her attention.

Doctor. How's he doing?

He's going to be fine. The MRI doesn't show any signs of serious injury, a mild concussion, that's all. We'll keep him overnight for observation and for the sedation to wear off and then you can take him home tomorrow morning.

The doctor reaches down and pet's Gidget on the head as he's talking to me. I hear her heave a big sigh. She's just happy to hear the love of her life is going to be OK.

That's a relief.

He'll probably have a monster headache for a day or two but I'll send him home with some meds for that. And, no strenuous activity for the next week.

OK.

I look over at Dirk, who is looking at Marc with a frown on his face.

Sherriff. Everything OK?

Uh, well, for now. He glances up at the TV. The recorded press conference is still playing and he scowls as he reaches for the bedside control and click's off the TV.

What does that mean?

Well, there is something I need to talk with you about. Maybe now isn't the best time.

No, let's talk now. How about out in the hall.

I rise from my seat and we make for the hospital room door. I turn to Anne and tell her to stay put and I'll be right back. She seems happy to stay by Marc's bed and hold his hand. Once in the hall, I cross my arms, hugging myself. I have a feeling I'm not going to like what I'm about to hear.

Ok, Dirk. What's Up?

Well, the crime lab over in Savannah just sent over the results of their initial analysis on that shell casing you and Marc found. And, there were no recognizable prints on it, as you said.

And?

And, you were right, it was a gun that was pushed down in the sand next to where Joe's body was found.

And?

And, there weren't any prints on the outside of the gun. But, there was a serial number on the gun.

And?

And, it's registered to Marc.

WHAT?

The gun found at the site of the body is Marc's?

Wow. I don't even know what to say to that. He keeps it in a drawer in our bedside table. Haven't had any reason to get it out or use it or anything for a long time. I can't imagine he even knew it was gone.

Who all knows about this gun?

Well, just him and me and...well, maybe...I don't know. There's no reason for anyone else to even know he has one.

As I'm speaking, a part of my brain is screaming for me to shut the fuck up. OK. Marc's gun, lawfully owned and registered to him is found buried in the sand next to a dead body and I'm telling the sheriff investigating the crime that only Marc and I even knew of its existence. Bad, Amy! Bad, girlfriend! Think! you idiot. Who else might've known about the gun?

Well, you know Sheriff, the gun was properly registered. So, anyone and everyone in your office who has access to that paperwork would know he owned it. Then, he has a conceal carry permit so he's got to go to the gun range periodically to qualify to maintain that permit. So, everyone at the County Sheriff's Office firing range would also be aware of it.

Uh huh. I see.

Do you? I mean do you understand that even if Marc's gun was found at the crime scene, that doesn't mean he did it, right? No one locks their doors. Anyone on this island could've come into our house, rummaged around, found and taken it. Look what just happened to us. It's not completely outside the realm of possibility.

Right. But...

But, damn it. NO!

Listen, Amy, calm down. I have to tell you something else.

What?

The gun was loaded with a round chambered and it'd been recently fired. Luckily, we did retrieve some fingerprints off of the bullets in the magazine.

OK.

I'm waiting for the other shoe to drop.

They belong to you.

Thunk!

I'm afraid I'm going to have to ask you to come down to the jail and answer some more questions. And, I'm leaving my deputy here to guard Marc and when he's discharged tomorrow, I'll be bringing him in for questioning as well.

You know, you were very much right on the money earlier today when you said finding that gun would yield some clues that would further my investigation. Very helpful indeed.

CHAPTER 11

Marc.

Marc!

MARC!!

WHAT?

Stop pacing. There's nothing you can do.

I hold out my hand to him.

Come here and sit down next to me for a minute.

No! Amy. I need to get the HELL out of this cell.

Marc grabs the cell door and shakes it as hard as he can.

SHERIFF! Do you hear me? THIS IS INSANE! WE DID NOT KILL JOE!

Marc yells toward the outer office at the Sheriff as he continues shaking the locked cell door for the millionth time.

Marc? Do you see this here roll of duct tape?

Sheriff Bentley comes to the doorway between the outer office and the cell block, holding a giant roll of black Gorilla brand duct tape.

If you don't simmer down, I'm going to put it to a new use and duct tape your mouth SHUT! Do you hear me? I mean it. If you don't sit down and shut up, I'm going to duct tape you to that there bench in that cell. Now, I mean it! Settle down!

I rise and walk to the cell and push my face thru the bars.

Sheriff, listen. You can't really be serious thinking Marc and I had anything to do with Joe's killing. You know you can trace Marc's movements last Saturday morning and I can pretty much account for all my time, too.

Then please explain to me how Marc's Baretta M9 pistol came to be found buried in the sea oats not 5 feet from where Joe's body was found. With your prints on the bullets inside the magazine.

Crickets…

Uh huh. That's what I thought. Now both of you SHUT UP! I'm afraid I'm going to have to insist you both exercise your right to remain silent.

CHAPTER 12

OK princesses, get out.

Earlier this morning, while the nurse was preparing Marc's discharge from the hospital, deputy sheriff Michael Matthews came to Marc's room and told us we needed to come with him down to the Sheriff's office for questioning. Anne and Gidget and I had all spent the night at the hospital with Marc and when Michael escorted us out, Anne had taken Gidget home, fed and walked her and left her in the house for the day we'd spend at the jail.

We were brought to a cell down at the Sheriff's office and told to wait there. Hard to refuse when the door was slammed and locked behind us. While we weren't actually charged with anything or processed for arrest, I've had occasion in the past to know that in the state of Georgia, we could actually be held for up to 48 hours for questioning. (That too is a story for another time.) So, we've both been pretty antsy at the prospect of not being able to go home anytime soon.

Marc said he was feeling pretty good, having had 18 plus hours of sedative-induced sleep in a comfy hospital bed. But, I'm feeling pretty rough having slept in an uncomfy chair next to his bed, awakened every fifteen minutes by someone coming in throughout the night to check on him. I've got a headache brewing and I haven't had a bath since Sunday morning before we took our investigative walk on the beach. Needless to say, I was feeling restless and anxious to get home.

Now it's late afternoon and Sheriff Bentley is unlocking the cell door and telling us we're free to go. I'm very annoyed and ask:

Um, Sherriff? Explain please.

D.A. says to cut you loose. While the gun belonging to you, Marc, and Amy's prints on the bullets in the magazine are compelling reasons to hold you both for questioning, the final results of the autopsy and the body's livor mortis place the actual time of death between ten pm and midnight, when Marc and I were drinking at Huca poos. That makes me Marc's alibi.

And since you, Amy, were caught on camera violating more than one of our traffic laws speeding through a red light on Butler in front of Stingray's restaurant at that same time, an arrest of either of you is out of the question.

So…Out! He demands as he waves his thumb toward the exit.

Marc is looking at me sideways, I'm sure wanting to know what I was doing out speeding through town between eleven and midnight. Marc leans over and whispers to me in his Ricky Ricardo falsetto:

Rucy, you got some 'splainin to do.

Marc and I slowly get to our feet, both of us stiff from sitting all day. We collect our belongings from Lucy, my straw bag with drone and ipad contents along with Marc's wallet and cell phone.

We sign the receipt for our stuff and Marc uses his phone to call his daughter, Anne, to come pick us up at the jail. We wait patiently in the lobby and Anne arrives about 20 minutes later. She seems both relieved and happy to ferry us back home.

Once home, Gidget greets us at the front door, barking wildly at the sound of Anne's car in the driveway. Her bark is so loud, we can hear it clearly from the road.

I feel relieved entering our home and Gidgie girl is all over us, kissing and sniffing us suspiciously. She's clearing her throat like she has a cough, and I know what she really wants is to question me about the events of the day, smelling as we do like concrete, criminals and a metal urinal. I kneel down and hug her close and whisper in her ear:

Not now...

Hey Marc, what do you think about goin' round to Rodney's and bringing him back here. I'm concerned about him bein' in that trailer alone, trying to fend for himself. I'll cook up a big pot of chili and some jalapeno cornbread and we'll all have a good meal and a cold beer.

Yeah, I was thinking the same thing. I think I'll pack up some of his clothes and he can camp out in our guest house for a while until we figure some things out.

Rodney's future on the island, the only home he's ever known, is very uncertain now that he's all alone in the world.

Anne, honey? Why don't you go with your Dad and help him with Rodney. Just hang out on the front stoop until Marc can assess Rodney's situation inside.

Sure. OK. Let's go Dad. I'll drive.

Yep. Yep. Yep.

As Marc and Anne get ready to go collect Rodney and bring him back to our home and care, Gidget's ears perk up and her tail curls over her back. She understands this is a chance for her and I to catch up and she's practically bursting at the seams to get the details of the day.

Once Marc is out the door and I hear Anne's car back out of the driveway, I turn to Gidget and fill her in on what happened after she left the hospital with Anne. She is curious about how Marc's gun escaped from his bedside table and under what circumstances my prints could've gotten on the bullets inside the gun's magazine.

Just now, I'm remembering that about a month ago, when Marc had to requalify for his conceal carry permit, he had invited me along to the shooting range. It would've been his idea of a romantic date but for the fact he'd invited Rodney to come along with us, telling me that as long as we had a gun in the house, he wanted to make sure I knew how to safely load and use it. It's actually more than just click boom. He taught me how to release the magazine, load bullets against the strong spring, and how to chamber a round by pulling back the slide. I'm confident that's how my prints got on the bullets. I'd fired his gun that day but not since and I'd actually sort of forgotten that the thing was hidden in the drawer of the Georgian chest next to Marc's side of the bed.

Aahh. Yeah. That makes sense. Did the Sheriff happen to say anything about who else he's been questioning?

Um. No, not really. But there are a few folks I can think of who had good enough reasons to wish him ill. But, honestly, I can't really see any of them actually doing the deed.

Really? Like who?

Well, Rodney for one. Certainly Joe has neglected and abused him, selling his prescription meds and making his life unnecessarily miserable. But Rodney's not very physically strong and in a confrontation with Joe would most certainly come out on the losing end of things. If Rodney did have a hand in Joe's death, he'd have to have had help. And who that would be I can't imagine.

Then there's Darla McClure whose son died of a drug overdose off Rodney's meds Joe sold him. To which Gidgie gave a little whimper:

Yeah, I remember seeing her at the funeral. I've never seen a human so abjectly sad and totally broken. And when I went up to her and she petted me, she left the most frightening smell on my fur. It's hard to explain, but it was kinda like desperation mixed with sleep deprivation and hopelessness. Honestly, I'm surprised she hasn't died of a broken heart. And her husband wouldn't even look at me. He just stood there looking down into that hole in the ground as their son was lowered down into it. I heard him whisper he wished he could just jump in it.

Yes. It was beyond tragic. Their son was their only child and now they're all alone in this world. But, they seem more hopeless than violent. It's hard to imagine those two actually shooting someone and then ramming a fence plank in Joe's head.

Gidget puts her paw on my knee. She's had an idea.

Maybe a drug deal gone bad. That Jesse Blankenship who attacked Marc looked in pretty bad shape when we saw him at the hospital. And I'm sure those "friends" he was buying those drugs for are probably not exactly upstanding, law abiding citizens.

Right. To which I add:

And, you know Lucy – over at the Sheriff's office – she once told me that Joe was the father of Micki Hucca poos' daughter.

It was one of those girls' nights out after Darla's son died. We had invited Darla out for drinks to take her mind off things and we'd had a couple of Micki's Friday night special extra large double strong cherry bombs. Micki was serving us and Darla had commented about how lucky Micki was to still have Taika, her daughter, even if she was one of them gays. Made no difference to her, live and let live was her motto. But still it must've been beyond hard to raise a kid like that in a place like Tybee, all alone with no money and no prospects. Folks talkin' and bein' mean the way they can be.

Not sure what all transpired there, but there's definitely been a lot of bad blood between The Sisters and Joe. More than once I've seen Joe in Hucca poos taunting Taika, yelling at her and calling her names, saying he didn't want Taika waiting on him or handling his food. He even got so out of hand one time when Marc and I were there that Marc had to get up from our table and go over to Joe and strong arm him out of the place.

Just one more time when Marc's military training had come in handy.

I don't think we're all that short of people who are probably happy to see the end of ole Joe.

But how can we find out who did it?

Good question, Gidgie girl. We're gonna have to noodle on that a little.

CHAPTER 13

Marc and Anne arrive back with Rodney in tow. I hear their voices and a kerfuffle as they stumble inside and a loud bang as someone slams the front door. Gidgie and I are in the kitchen, and while she would normally run to the front door, barking, she's too pre-occupied with the smell of my chili and the prospect of a bean or a morsel of meat falling to the floor.

I wipe my hands on a dishtowel and come from the kitchen into the family room where Marc and Rodney are gingerly depositing themselves on one of the sofas. Marc is still sore from the attack yesterday and Rodney seems a bit more unsteady than usual on his feet and crutches. Rodney has muscular dystrophy and seizures and ambulates on crutches with difficulty under the best of circumstances. But, tonight he seems particularly frail as if he's had to run a marathon or hike a trail and his twisted legs are about to give way underneath him.

Marc picks up the remote control and switches on the TV. There's an Atlanta Hawks game on tonight and we'll spend our evening enjoying our dinner in the family room while watching Trae Young rack up his usual double-double. Gidgie has followed me into the family room and as Anne makes her way to the kitchen to help out with serving dinner to the guys, she pets Gidget on the head and tells her hello.

Gidget has decided to greet Rodney, bumping his hand with her nose and placing her Pyr paw gently on his arthritic knee, welcoming him to our home. She absolutely knows and loves Rodney. She seems to understand that his frailty means he needs her care and protection. So, an honorary member of her pack he has become.

The Hawks pre-game show has started and Anne and I dish up the chili and grab a cold beer from the fridge for Marc. Rodney can't drink alcohol because of all the meds he's supposed to be taking and I can't stand the taste of beer. I leave it to Anne to decide what she wants. It's so incredibly nice to have Anne spend the evening with us and the thought ocurrs to me that maybe I should call Tyler and see if he can come over too. I mention this to Marc and he says he'd already called Tyler and he's on duty tonight and can't make it.

So we're set for the night and I ask Anne if she wants to stay over. She does. I tell Rodney the guest house just off the back porch walk is all ready for him and he smiles and says thank you. He asks if Gidgie can stay with him out there and I glance at her and she nods her head once and I say:

Sure, she'd be happy to stay with you. I'm sure this whole business with Joe has been very unsettling for you and she'll keep watch over things.

The Hawks are workin' real hard to loose against the Knicks and about two hours later, we're all done for the night. Anne, who is not crazy about basketball has already gone up to the guest room and now Marc is helping Rodney make his way to the guest house. I brought in his clothes while Marc helped clean up the dinner dishes, putting them on the kitchen counter directly over the dish washer. Unbelievable! Is that a man thing?

Anyway, Rodney and Marc, escorted, by Gidgie shamble their way slowly out the back door as I load the dishes into the dishwasher. I glance out the kitchen bay window and see the lights go on in the guest house and I hear Marc yell:

Godnight. Watch over Rodney, Gidgie girl.

She woofs once.

What a busy few days. I'm dog tired and after I wipe down the counter and put the chili pan in the sink to soak, I make my way upstairs to our bedroom.

A few minutes later, Marc opens the bedroom door, comes in while removing his shirt and unbuckling his pants. He climbs in bed and I roll on my side to lay up close to him, stretching out my legs the full length of his strong, warm body and deeply breath in his comforting smell. I don't even remember going to sleep.

CHAPTER 14

The next morning, I wake up to the smell of bacon and coffee. Dear Lord, this truly is paradise.

I slowly make my way to the bathroom and start the shower. The water is steaming hot and all I want to do is stand under its pounding comfort all day. Afterward, I dress and brush my teeth and start making my way down to the kitchen. Anne and Marc are already at the table and I hear the front door open and in walks Tyler, just coming off his shift at the fire department. With Rodney eventually making his morning appearance, our lovely little family is all together around the kitchen table, chitter chattering and laughing and planning our days.

Marc is still at loose ends with the continued moratorium on his flying. Anne will be going to work soon at E. Shavers book store – otherwise know by the locals as the kitty cat bookstore because of the two fat and fluffy strays who live there. Tyler will be going home to sleep, with his next duty scheduled for the night shift again tonight. I plan to work on my book and spend the day writing.

Gidget, who has come in with Rodney, walks up to me and greets me by sniffing my butt.

Honestly, Gidget, you don't know it's me?!

She looks me in the eye and starts cutting her eyes toward the family room. Back and forth, my eyes to the family room back to my eyes back to the family room. Clearly she's signally me to meet her in the family room. I grab a cup of coffee from the pot and pop a piece of bacon in my mouth and exit the kitchen, turning on the TV and tuning it to Good Morning America. I sit on the sofa and look at Gidget who has jumped up next to me. She leans in close and when I'm sure no one can hear us, I whisper to her:

Ok, girlie. What's up?

Well, last night after we all went to bed, Rodney made a phone call. I don't know who he was talking to but what he said was very weird.

Weird like how?

Well, he said something like, "No, I don't think so. No one's asked me anything except the last time I saw him. "

And then:

"you probably oughta go back home until this all blows over. No, no, there's no need. I'm staying with Marc and Amy for a while. But, they spent all day yesterday at the Sheriff's being questioned. I'm very worried they might be getting caught up in this. And I'm not sure what to do about that. No. Don't! I'm Ok. Just go back to Syracuse and don't try and contact me. I'll call you if there are any new developments. For now, it's no news is good news."

Wow! That's strange.

Yeah, And Rodney's smellin' kinda strange too. And not just his normal smells. It's sort of like a mix of funky fear, relief and…um, I dunno…old spice, maybe?

Funky fear?

Yeah, you know. Fear, not for himself. Fear something bad is about to happen to someone he cares about.

Hmmm.

At this precise moment, I hear Marc clear his throat right behind my right ear. I'd been so intent on what Gidget was saying, I didn't even realize Marc had come from the kitchen. How long he'd been standing behind me while Gidget and I were talking I don't know. I turn around and Marc is staring quizzically into my eyes, then he looks at Gidget, his mouth dropping open. For the first time in his life, he is speechless. And, I too don't know exactly what to say. So, he and Gidget and I all just continue to stare at each other.

After a few seconds, I say:

Honey, maybe you better sit down and let me try to explain.

Ummm. Yeah. OK. Pls Splain.

Marc moves to the other sofa, sits leaning forward, arms on his knees. He's rubbing his forehead, waiting for me to explain.

Ok. Now, I know you're going to be surprised by this. But, Gidget can talk.

Uh huh.

She started talking to me about a week after she came to live with us.

Uh huh.

I didn't tell you – or anyone – because I thought you might think I had come unhinged. And, Gidget said she was ok keeping it as our little secret and we agreed to let the universe sort it all out later. So, I…I guess it's later.

To which Gidget yells:

Surprise!

Ssshhhh! We three look around toward the kitchen. But, everyone is still talking and eating and apparently no one has heard.

Ok so what am I supposed to do with this information.

Ummm. Nothing I guess. I whisper. Except maybe keep it just between us. I'm not sure what people would think – or maybe do – if this was known.

Yeah. Um. Ok. I'm not sure I'd want to tell anyone this anyway and have everyone thinking I'm unhinged. Now what?

Well, Gidget was just telling me about a phone call of Rodney's she overheard last night. Tell Marc what you just told me.

Gidget repeats verbatim the conversation she overheard and Marc, too, thinks something is fishy. He suggests that he talk to Rodney about this when he can get him alone in the guest house.

But how will you explain how you know about this conversation without revealing your source is Gidget?

Yeah, that's a puzzlement. I'll have to think about it.

Marc rises from the sofa and returns to the kitchen, taking his usual place in the captain's chair at the head of the table.

Gidget jumps down and follows Marc into the kitchen, where she takes up her usual place next to his chair. She is so tall that her chin clears the table's edge and I know she's waiting to scarf a bit of bacon off Marc's plate the moment he's not looking. Before she can make her move, Marc breaks off a piece of crispy bacon from one of his two rashers and places it on the table in front of Gidget's nose, which she promptly grabs, smacking loudly and licking her lips in delight.

I'm still sitting on the sofa with my coffee, pretending to watch GMA. I feel very unsettled at the moment. But, I know Marc will figure something out.

CHAPTER 15

I'm in the kitchen, cleaning up after breakfast. Anne and Tyler have said their goodbyes and Marc is asking Rodney if he needs help getting himself together for the day. I'm watching them through the kitchen window as they make their way across the garden and into the guest-house, where Marc will help Rodney straighten up, bathe and dress and will somehow address the issue of his strange nocturnal phone call.

I'm anxious to know the scoop. I wait about fifteen minutes and then decide I can't wait one more minute and, surely by now, Rodney is dressed and ready to receive visitors. So, I walk out to the guest house and knock on the door. Marc opens it and ushers me in. Rodney is sitting at the small kitchen table next to the window, looking dejected, forehead in hand, eyes cast to his feet.

I move to the empty kitchen chair across from Rodney and I look at Marc for some signal as to where we are in this conversation and how he's chosen to broach the subject of Rodney's telephone call.

So, what's the plan for today? I ask looking toward Rodney.

I think I need to talk to Sherriff Bentley.

Oh, really? What about honey?

The investigation into Joe's death.

I see, I say as I glance at Marc.

Marc nods his head once.

Can we take you down to his office?

No, I think I'll call him first and see where we can meet. Maybe Huca poo's.

I see. Ok then, honey. We'll leave you to it. Maybe we can all meet down at Huca poos a little later for an early dinner.

Yeah, maybe.

CHAPTER 16

Marc and I are sitting in Huca poo's, in a booth in the back corner by the window, eating two of the Sisters giant cheese pizza slices. Marc is having a cherry bomb. I'm having water. The sun is just beginning to sink into the sea and there's a warm, rosy glow all through the joint. I'm looking at Marc and thinking for the millionth time how handsome he is and how lucky I am to be with him.

The door swings open to the gentle tinkle of the door chimes and in shuffles Rodney on his two forearm clutches. He stops and looks around for a second and spies us in the corner. I see him and wave him over. I scoot over a few inches so he knows I intend for him to sit next to me. I mouth "Rodney" to Marc, whose back is to the door and he turns and sees Rodney arrive at our table and watches him slide into the booth next to me. I slip my arm through his and give him a little hug and touch my cheek to his shoulder.

Rodney looks very serious this evening, his usual goofy infectious grin gone from his unshaven face. He looks a little gray in the rosy evening sunlight and I can tell he's clearly upset.

What's up, honey? I ask him. Did you talk to the Sherriff?

Yeah. I've decided to tell the Sheriff what I did.

Marc raises his eyebrows and glances sideways at me.

And what exactly are you planning on telling said Sheriff? Marc asks in his deceptively calm way.

That I killed Joe. I thought about what you said and how the honorable thing to do is to be a man and take responsibility for what I did. I hope I can explain why I did it and maybe there'll be some mercy. Truth is, I ain't got no real life out in this world now anyway, with no one to look after me. I can barely get around let alone take care of myself and get my meds and food and all. And...

Oh, Rodney. I lay my head on his shoulder and cover his hand with mine.

No, Amy. It's true.

Rodney pushes me away. He doesn't want sympathy and now is not a time for him to let his resolve weaken with emotion.

I can't take care of myself and if I'm in prison, at least I'll have a place to live and sleep and food and medicine. It'll actually be kind of a relief to be taken care of. And, I did kill Joe. I did pull the trigger and end his life. However much he deserved it. I killed him. And, that's that.

Micki Huca poo comes by our table with a water pitcher and I can tell by the look on her face that she's overheard some of what Rodney has just said and she looks very sad. She leans over the table and fills my water glass, catches my eye and for one split second I think I see tears welling in her eyes. Like everyone who knows Rodney, she deeply loves him and his gentle nature and funny sense of humor. And like everyone who knew Joe, she loathed him for his neglect and mistreatment of Rodney as well as for some of their own particular reasons. He was a bully and someone bereft of compassion and basic decency.

So now Micki knows our secret. That Rodney killed Joe and that Marc and I have known about it for some unknown period of time. And since Rodney is not already sitting in a cell, it's Information we clearly have kept secret and not shared with the Sheriff.

Micki turns on her heal and walks double quick back behind the counter and yells for Louise. I watch her go into the kitchen and through the order pick up window, I can see her and Louise talking animatedly about what I'm guessing is the situation at hand. Now there are five of us with a secret.

The front door bangs open as if someone has just tried to jerk it off its hinges. It bangs against the wall, the door chimes ring furiously and the sunglasses on the steer scull rattle. In strides Sheriff Dirk Bentley, scowling around the place for a full ten seconds while his eyes adjust to the dimmer lighting of the dinner, then he sees Rodney. Dirk walks right to our table and makes to sit in the booth next to Marc. He practically sits on Marc before Marc is able to move over to make room for our giant Sheriff.

OK. Rodney. I'm here. What is so all fired important I had to drop everything and meet you here.

Well, Sheriff. I need to tell you something.

OK, What?

Well…Sheriff, it's like this. Rodney hesitates.

Like what, Rodney?

Rodney is loosing his nerve. Suddenly the reality of actually confessing to a murder in a state that still has the death penalty is dawning on him. He's pinning his hopes on the killing being justifiable – which it most certainly was – on receiving mercy from the court – which he most certainly deserves – and being given a life sentence in a comfy minimum security prison – which is a most uncertain outcome at best.

Well, What damn it. Spit it out?

Dirk is raising his voice now as his patience is thinning.

Out of the corner of my eye, I see Micki come out from the kitchen and make an empty-handed b-line for Michael Matthews, who is sitting at the counter. Leaning her ample bosom over the counter she frantically whispers something in his ear, to which he whips his head around and looks right at our little group. I can tell, we are now six secret keepers.

So, I say:

Uh Sheriff. Listen, I think what Rodney is trying to get at is he's concerned about what's happening with your investigation into Joe's death. Ever since you announced it was actually a murder, everyone's been on pins and needles wondering if there's a killer among us. I glance at Marc and nod my head slightly toward the kitchen. He raises his eyebrows and widens his eyes at me, as if asking:

"What?"

God, it would be so helpful right now if Marc and I had that psychic connection common of deeply bonded couples and I could just put my thoughts into his head. But, we are not yet that closely bonded and he remains clueless as to what is going on behind him.

And, turns out there is quite a lot going on behind the backs of Marc and the Sheriff. Michael, who Micki just whispered to, has pulled out his cell phone and is dialing furiously.

Though it must've been several minutes, it seemed like only seconds pass before Darla McClure comes rushing into Huca poo's, looking immediately in our direction and scurrying over to the counter and huddling with Michael and Micki and Louise, who has now come out from the kitchen to join the growing crowd at the counter. Clearly we are now seven secret keepers. Rodney, Marc, and me, Micki, Louise, Michael, and Darla.

What the hell is going on I can't even begin to guess.

Rodney takes a deep breath and says,

No Sheriff that's not what I was wanting to talk to you about. What I need to tell you is…

Yeeesss.

I killed Joe.

WHAT?

Dirk jumps up from the booth.

What the FUCK Rodney?

All 6'4" of him is now towering over Rodney, his thumb instinctively flicks the snap on his gun holster, one hand resting on his hip, the other hand on the grip of his Glock 22 service pistol.

Rodney looks frail and small under the big man's looming form and his voice is shaking a little.

Yes. Yes. It was me. I shot him in the head with Marc's gun. And then Jim and Sara Berberian helped me cover it up.

Jim and who?

Jim and Sara Berberian. They're my friends from central NY. You know, that couple who comes down here to Tybee to spend the winter. Over the years, we've become friends and, well, one day…right here in Huca Poos… we started talking about things and we just kinda decided it was time Joe met his maker.

Oh, Rodney, I say.

Amy, you know better than most Joe was a cruel, uncaring sorry excuse for a human being. He was my uncle and I can still remember how much my mama loved him. But, he never amounted to nothin', always looking for the quickest way to make a buck, legal or not, and he didn't care who he hurt in the process.

He only grudgingly looked after me after mama died and only then 'cause l was gettin' some money from the gov'ment every month. And, I knew he was stealing my phenobarbitals and pain meds and sellin' em. When I heard Darla's son died of that overdose, I knew it was my drugs Joe had stolen and sold to him. I felt so damn bad about that, but what could I have done to stop him? He was a brute and if I'd said anything to anyone he'd probly've beat me to death just for spite.

And, I knew about his trying to take Huca poo's away from the sisters. I don't know if you know this or not, but Joe was the father of Micki's daughter. He always said that little lesbo cunt was a mistake and should've been aborted. He'd even given Micki some money back then to end it, which – apparently – Micki had used instead to invest in buying Huca poo's. I don't know how Joe found that out but he told me once he was glad Micki had used the money "not for its intended purpose" because now he could use that fact to try and lay a claim to some ownership in Huca poo's. I don't exactly understand all the legal ins and outs but he'd seen a lawyer over in Savannah and he seemed to think he could win a court judgment for at least some ownership interest in the place and that the dough would start rollin' in and we'd be set for life.

Then, about a month ago, I overhead him on the phone talkin' to somebody about the turtles and how he could get his hands on some of them eggs and maybe even catch a pregnant mama turtle while she

91

was laying those eggs. He could not have been more excited about how much money those turtles and their babies could fetch. Marc had bought me some data minutes for my phone and I went on the internet and googled about loggerhead sea turtles and found out the horrible things some of those people over in Asia do to those poor animals, even while they're still alive, and I just couldn't believe that even Joe would be willing to be a part of something like that. It just sounded too horrifying even for him.

But, one night last September after he'd been out drinking, he came home and actually had one of them turtle eggs. He took it in the kitchen, used a boning knife and sliced it open. Inside was a perfectly formed little turtle. I don't know if it was ready to hatch or not, but it was moving a little. Joe pinched its neck and held onto its little head, took that boning knife and sliced it's head right off. That little thing's head didn't come clean off and Joe had to sort of saw it off, blood and goo oozing all over as it struggled and flailed. When I saw that I knew then I had to do something to stop his evil in this world.

But, I didn't really know how to go about killin' him. I'd made friends with an older couple, Jim and Sara Berberian, who regular come down to Tybee for the winter and one afternoon, right here in Huca poo's, we were sittin' in that both right over there and I just started blathering on about Joe and some of the things he'd done and was about to do. And then Sara actually said, sounds like he was someone who needed killing.

I was just so stunned that someone else would actually see things the same way I did and it made me start thinking that, well now, maybe Joe did need killing. And, how maybe it just might be the right thing to do to rid this world of him. So I just said to her, supposin' someone had a mind to actually get rid of Joe, could she imagine how in the world that might be done.

For the rest of the afternoon, Jim and Sara and I sat her in Huca poo's, thinkin' on it and talkin' bout it. And, I think it was Jim that said the only sure fire way to ensure Joe would be dead and not somehow recover and come after me, would be if he was shot in the head. Dead as a door nail. No way back from a bullet in the ole brain. But, then there'd prob'ly need to be a cover for the bullet, so it wouldn't look like that was the actual cause of death. You know, sort of muddy the waters and make it harder for the police to figure out who did it. We actually talked about the pros and cons of maybe cutting off his head. But, then the problem would be disposing of it. It all just sounded too compli- cated and impossible until Sara suggested something maybe could be rammed in his scull and make it look like that was the cause of death, hiding the bullet wound. And Jim seemed to think that was a good idea if it could be made to look like a freak accident or something. But we'd have to think on it some more to figure it all out.

It was gettin' on toward dusk and I needed to start makin' my way back to the trailer. I don't walk so good and after dark it's hard to see. So, Jim and Sara and I agreed we'd meet up for lunch in two days time back here at Huca poo's and that it would be my job to think of where and how I could get my hands on a gun. Jim and Sara's job was to figure out a way to cover up the bullet wound and make it look like an accident.

And, this is where I need to say I'm mighty sorry to you and Amy, Marc.

Rodney turns to Marc and nods a little and says,

The only person I could even think might actually have a gun I could get my hands on was you, Marc. I didn't know for sure but I figured with you being ex-military, maybe you might've had one. So, last week I decided I'd just drop by your house. I knew you guys never lock your doors, like everyone else who lives here and if you weren't home, I'd just poke around a little. And sure enough, the day I came by you were both out and the front door was open, so I just let myself in. Once inside, I really didn't know where to start lookin'. But I tried to think like you and I figured if you had a gun, you'd have it to protect your fambily and if you had to get your hands on it quick like it'd have to be close at hand in the night. So, night stand…and sure enough…I found that 9mm in your nightstand drawer.

God, I was so scared. It was weird, almost like watching some-one else's hand reaching in the drawer. And, I did actually think twice about taking it. You guys have always been so good to me. Marc, you've always been more like my brother than just a friend. And I did feel bad 'bout potentially involving you by using your gun. Then, I remem-bered the sight of that tiny baby turtle squirming and flailing in it's shell as Joe sawed off it's head. And, I just thought I had no choice. I'd come this far. I had to keep going. I took your gun. The magazine was already in it. And I remembered what you taught me that time I went with you and Amy to the shotting range to qualify to keep your con-ceal carry permit. How to release the safety, pull the slide to chamber a round and how to aim and fire without shooting yourself. I tucked it in my pants pocket and left.

I think you probly know the rest. Last Thursday it became clear the hurricane was changing course and heading our way. Jim and Sara said we should plan to kill Joe on Friday night when the storm would be blowing through. We'd have to wait for the eye to pass over Tybee so it'd be calm enough to lure him out to the beach and do the deed. They seemed to think the storm might provide some cover for what we were about to do. At the very least the wind and rain would wipe out any of our footprints. If we got lucky, maybe a tidal surge would actually pick up his body and wash it out to sea. 'Course that didn't happen, the storm weakened too much coming cross the state so the surge wasn't strong enough and the dead weight of his body got tangled in the sea oats.

Rodney has been talking for about a half hour and we're all speechless at what we are hearing.

Rodney, our frail, crippled, loving, happy go lucky dear, dear friend, conceived, planned and executed the cold blooded murder of his uncle, Joe Smith. A task none of us would've ever thought he'd have been capable of doing. Granted, he had a little help from his friends. But, Joe's murder had been Rodney's show from the beginning. I guess you never really know what a person is capable of until that person is pushed past their limits. All those years Joe was neglecting and using and abusing Rodney and Rodney had said not one word against his uncle. He'd let Joe steal his medications which he badly needed just to survive. He'd tolerated the less than adequate food and filthy living conditions Joe provided. He'd leaned on Marc and me and others for some of the basic necessities like bathing and clean clothes and transportation to doctors appointments, a humiliation I could now see deeply grieved him. But, hurting others by dealing drugs, abandoning his child and her mother all those years ago and now trying to use that connection to take Huca poo's away from the sisters, and then exploiting the helpless turtles and their torture and suffering for money was all the last straws Rodney could bear and he'd decided something had to be done and that he was the only one who could do it.

Dirk is hesitating now. He's not really sure what to do next. Rodney is physically frail, is not about to try and make a break for it and Dirk isn't used to not having to man handle a suspect. But, his training kicks in and he says:

OK, Rodney. I need you to stand up and put your hands behind your back.

Rodney slowly pushes himself out of the booth, slipping his arms into his forearm crutches and struggling up onto his feet. As he's making to turn around and trying to balance himself against the side of the booth so he can put his hands behind his back, Micki comes rushing over to our table.

Sheriff? Wait! What are you doing?

Now, Miss Huca poo, this is police business, please don't interfere. Rodney here has just confessed to Joe's murder and I'm arresting him.

Well, that is patently absurd, Sheriff! I mean even you can see Rodney is not physically strong enough to hurt a fly. I, on the other hand, could've snapped that good for nothing calamari butt hole like a twig. And I had good reason to hate both his literal and his proverbial guts, as you and everyone else on this island well knows. And, last Friday night, I just decided it was as good a time as any to put me and this whole island out of our misery by ending his sorry, shit kicking life.

What?

No, Sheriff, Micki is lying.

Louise has now come from around the counter to stand next to Rodney, her arm draped around his shoulder.

Micki was here at the diner last Friday evening 'til closing. You and Marc were here downing those double-strong cherry bombs she makes. I slipped out the back and met Joe down on the dunes and I shot him.

I hated him mightily for the way he treated Micki and he was threatening to take us to court and get some sort of court ordered ownership interest in this place because of the money he'd given Micki all those years ago when Mikki was pregnant with his child. She'd used that money to help me buy this place and it's all we've got in this world. He was a money-grubbing, son of a bitch and if he'd gotten any sort of ownership in this place, he'd have bled it and us dry and we'd be left with nothing. And look at us, we're both too old to start over now, either here on Tybee or anywhere else. I couldn't let him destroy the only thing we have in this world that keeps us (and a few others around here) alive. I just couldn't let that happen.

I knew Friday night would be uber busy what with the storm blowing through and every islander who'd refused to evacuate in here riding out the storm, downing Micki's Friday night special double-strong cherry bombs. I called the old ass hole and told him I wanted to meet and talk about a settlement of the ownership issue and I'd be willing to give him a percentage of our weekly takings if he'd meet me to talk it through. He couldn't have been more eager.

I told him to meet me on the dune near that rancid trailer of his at 11:00pm, when I knew Micki and Huca poo's would be busiest. I slipped out a little before then and just sort of sat down in the sea oats and waited for him. He, of course, staggered along, drunk as usual, at our agreed time and I just stood up and popped a cap in his sorry melon head.

I'm shocked to see Louise smile a little and begin to laugh quietly to herself. The more she tried not to the harder she laughed, letting out a little pig snort before covering her mouth and saying:

Sorry…but you should've seen the look of total surprise and shock on his fucking little shit face when I shot him.

For the millionth time in the last forty eight hours, I am shocked and flabbergasted and speechless. And, I'm not the only one. The whole place is dead quiet. After a few seconds, Michael Matthews spins round on his counter stool and stands up.

Well, now. That can't be right. Since I was the one who shot Joe. I was on the dunes, turtle watching, trying to help those little itty bitty newly hatched baby turtles get to the sea when Joe came stomping along the shore with his mega godzilla feet. Louise is right, he was drunk, stomping around, yelling about how the little bastards had ruined him and cost him his fortune. But, he had a plan to fix all that. He was stomping on the babies trying to crush and break their shells and kill them. I was so enraged, I lost my head and I pulled out my pistol and plugged a hole in his fat head.

Darla turned around on her stool and got to her feet and walked over to our table. Sheriff. I don't know what these idiots are talking about, because I shot Joe. I found out he was the one who sold the oxycontin pills to my son, the ones he took and killed hisself. I owed it to myself and his father to return the favor and end Joe's life. I'm the one who shot and killed Joe.

I started to say something too but Marc kicked my shin under the table and shook his head.

No, Amy. This is for the Island to do.

But.

No.

I relaxed back into my seat. Marc was right. We'd been here on Tybee long enough to have put down some roots, to have close friends who care for us, and for us to have fallen in love with the Island and to consider it our home. But, we weren't born and raised here and there's a special unbreakable bond between those who were. Like between Rodney and the Sisters and Michael and Darla. And, it was for them to decide how best to address the issue of who was going to be held accountable for Joe's murder.

Well now, if that doesn't beat all. I got one murder and five killers all eagerly confessing to it. I bet that's gotta be some kinda record. And, just what am I supposed to do with all these confessions. You couldn't all have killed Joe. But, you all seem to think you each had a compelling motive and the opportunity to do the deed.

Well, Sheriff.

Marc is now chiming in, using his most reasonable military tone of voice that Dirk would recognize and respect.

You probably ought to talk to the county prosecutor and deliver all five confessions and see what he has to say. I don't think you can arrest five different people for the same single crime.

Unless it was a conspiracy.

A conspiracy to do what? All confess to the same murder in a death penalty state? Who in their right mind would do that?

Who in deed?

Dirk turns and scowls at each of the confessors in turn.

Well, Sheriff, it seems to me that Marc is right. The best thing would be to take all this to the prosecutor and see what he says is the best course of action. In the meantime, maybe you could let Rodney come home with Marc and me and we'll keep an eye on him for you.

Dirk slowly rubs his stubbled chin and considers my offer for a moment. He knows the prosecutor isn't going to want to bring charges against Rodney, anyway. There's not enough evidence to prove it was Rodney and no one else who killed Joe. And, four other compelling confessions would be enough reasonable doubt at trial for a jury to find Rodney not guilty. And, any jury formed from Tybee's residents would be beyond sympathetic to Rodney and happy to find a legal reason to let him go free. So, there's no point in taking Rodney into custody and locking him up. Plus, Rodney has some special physical needs that the local jail is not equipped to handle and it would be easier all the way around to release him into Marc's and my care.

Slowly, Dirk puts this all together and acquiesces to my suggestion and agrees to let Rodney come home with us. Marc and I slide out of the booth. I take Rodney by the arm and we slowly limp our way to the door, Marc walking ahead and opening the door for us. I pass by Micki and she and I catch each other's eye and she gives me a little wink and I return a tiny smile. Not enough gesture between us for anyone else to notice, but enough for she and I to know we now share a bond that can never be broken.

As Rodney and I cross the threshold of Huca poo's, I hear Dirk threaten those remaining,

Ok. Now listen up folks. I suspect I know what's really going on here and I can't say I blame you. But, if I ever get even a whimper of a whiff that any one of you has lied to me about killing Joe, I swear I will arrest you all for obstruction of justice faster than you can say Huca poo's. And, there's no statute of limitations on murder. So, whatever you all think you've accomplished here today, you better be prepared to live with for the rest of your lives. Got it?

Vague "uh huhs" are murmured behind our backs. I glance sideways at Rodney and I see a tear roll down his cheek. I take his arm and pull him close to me as we slowly take the stairs out of Huca poo's and out onto Tybee's warm evening sand, a soft ocean wind – blown clean and fresh from the passing of the storm – blowing in our faces. He knows I've seen.

His shaky whisper is in my ear:
It's just the sun is in my eyes.

AFTER

Marc and I are standing on the equator in Quito, Ecuador. It's Christmas Day and Marc – my lovely, brilliant nerd – has brought me and his Spot X GPS from the motor glider and we're standing at precisely Latitude 0-0-0 and Longitude 78-27'-8" on the raised round platform in front of the Mitad del Mundo obelisk, one of us on each side of the bright yellow line marking the middle of the world. And because it's December, the middle of the rainy season in Ecuador, we are also standing in a rain storm, getting soaked to the skin.

And contrary to Marc's custom, he has wrapped me tightly in his arms and is looking directly in my eyes, telling me how much he loves me. He reaches into his front pants pocket and produces the most beautiful sapphire and diamond ring I've ever seen. He slips it onto the third finger of my left hand and tells me:

Get yourself a dress, baby, we're getting married in May.

Apparently, I was wrong in my earlier assessment and it has crossed his mind to marry again and to make me his wife.

I am the happiest I have ever been.
And that's the end of this story.